Laurel Springs Book Two

LOVE'S CALL

AMANDA SPEIGHTS

HIGH PLAINS WOMAN
PRESS

To request permission please contact the author at hello@amandaspeights.com.
Library of Congress Control Number: 2025905540

Paperback: ISBN 979-8-9878676-2-4
Ebook: ISBN 979-8-9878676-3-1

Editor: Brittany Bookworm Author Services
Cover Design: Roseanna White Designs
Author Photo: Melissa DeMers

Publisher: High Plains Woman Press

www.AmandaSpeights.com

*To those who have loved deeply, lost profoundly,
and found the courage to love again.*

1

Ginny

1869 Sutton's Creek, Colorado Territory

A day may begin as any other, yet end like no other.

My eyes wander beyond Old Man Marshall, peering at everything and nothing all at once, searching for an escape from his words. The doorframe is rough under my hand as I brace to steady my wobbly knees. The lines on the old man's face are like the crevices of these very mountains, deep and rugged. His eyes hold a sorrow that penetrates me to my core, and I swallow back the bile that rises up my clenched throat. The trees beyond him are still. The dirt beneath his dusty boots is dry. I'm trapped, suffocating, and there's no escape. This isn't something I am able to break free from. My opposite hand clutches my blouse. It's too tight. The collar is choking me. Once again, my eyes shift to the despair on the man's face. An urge to hug him stirs within me. An urge to lift his sadness. But I can't. His grief isn't solely for himself, I know, it's mostly for me.

"Ginny." He steps forward and holds out his arm as if he's going to catch me when I fall.

I shake my head. This can't be. I eek out the words, "He was fine this morning. No. There's been a mistake. You're wrong. Where is he? I need to see him. He's all right, I'll show you. Whatever happened, I'll nurse him back to health."

Marsh catches my arm as I stumble past him. I need to get to my husband.

"Ginny. Jake's gone," he repeats, grasping my arm. His eyes are pleading with me to understand. "I'm so sorry, Ginny."

No. You're wrong goddamn it! You're wrong. Everyone knows Old Man Marshall's a drunk. I rush for the creek bed when Big Joe crests the bank with Jake slung over his shoulder, arms and legs limp and dangling.

My feet halt and a gasp escapes my lips. "No," I whisper. "No." My legs turn to jelly as my stomach begs to relieve itself of the breakfast Jake and I shared this very morning. I reach for something, anything, but there's nothing to grab onto. I crumble to the ground in disbelief of what's happening. My chest squeezes as tight as a rag wrung out in the wash.

Dust stirs as Joe gently lays Jake before me. "I'm sorry, Ginny," his voice is barely above a whisper.

Jake's shirt is soaked in blood, but it's his face I study. He can't be gone. He's only sleeping. He'll wake up and this will all be a nightmare. Is it wrong to touch him? My trembling hand hovers. It can't be. I need to touch him. I need to feel that he's real, that my life with him has always been real. Yet, the moment feels too sacred.

A shadow of whiskers covers his jaw, around his lips, and down his neck. When I shaved him on Sunday, I had no idea it would be the last time. When our naked bodies were entwined this morning, I had no idea it would be the last time.

My hand twitches as I slowly dare to touch him, laying a palm on his shoulder, still hesitant if this is all right to do. I slide my shaky fingers through his hair. His locks are soft between my fingers, as always. "I love you, Jake," I whisper as I rest my forehead against his. "I love you. I'll always love you."

It occurs to me that we're alone. The men have respectfully given me space.

"Why, God?"

The sky is the color of turquoise, and warmth from the sun envelops me. The earth doesn't cease to exist as it feels it should. It's a completely normal day for most folks. For everyone but me. I shout to the heavens, "You were supposed to bring him home to me today." Of course, I mean He was to bring him home *alive*. Jake was supposed to come through the door whistling, take me in his arms and give me a twirl as he does every day.

The answer comes without a face. *But Ginny, I brought him home to me.*

There's an instant relief and peace I can't explain if I try. Jake's in a more favorable place. I don't know how I know this, but I do. Which means the place they call hell doesn't exist. If it did, as we'd been raised to believe, Jake would be there because cussing, cardplaying, and whiskey drinking will surely send you into the lake of fire. But I clearly heard God tell me Jake's with Him.

I peer down at my husband's face, forever at rest. *I love you, Jake.* Pushing myself to my feet, I look to Big Joe, Old Man Marshall, and the other men, who solemnly lean against my cabin. I nod to let them know they can take Jake's body. With heavy feet, I turn and make my way towards the rippling water of the creek mere yards away.

I fix my eyes on the cross, perched at the top of the rocky mound in front of me. The men sing "Amazing Grace" while Lee gracefully runs the bow over the strings of his fiddle. For the first time, the weight of my circumstances tumbles over me. Jake is gone. He's never coming back.

My throat is thick as I push back the sobs that beg to come. The relief I felt at God's words have dissolved like sugar in boiling water. As hard as I try to be strong for Jake, my lips involuntarily quiver, and salty tears run down my cheeks. Big Joe hands me a handkerchief. I'm grateful but can't bring myself to look at him. I bury my face into the piece of cloth and let the pain, sadness, and loss wrack through my body. Joe's strong arms are wrapped around me as my head burrows into his chest. All pride is gone as I hide in the comfort of his embrace. There's a shrieking sound, a woman wailing. It's me. The sound is coming from me, and I can neither stop nor bother to care. I know Joe is holding me up because I can no longer stand on my own.

Jake is gone. I'll never see his smile, hear his laugh, or feel his arms around me again. My life will be forever different. All the dreams he and I had of children or growing old together have been snuffed out like the flame of a candle at bedtime.

Too weary to mourn any longer, I summon the strength to step out of Joe's embrace and away from the grave.

"Ginny?" He takes my arm.

I peer into his heartbroken eyes and force a smile. *I'm all right, just need rest.* I cup my hand over his to reassure him.

Once inside my cabin I lay on my bed, pull Jake's pillow to me, and take a deep inhale of his scent that still lingers. I wonder how long it'll stay. The ability to smell him while knowing he is gone forever is a surreal thought. "Oh, Jake, what happens now? How do I live without you?"

We'll figure it out, we always do. It's as if he whispers in my ear and his words soothe me.

I clutch the pillow more tightly, letting exhaustion wash over me and guide me into a deep, peaceful sleep.

2

Joe

Resting my elbows on my knees, the warped step of Jake and Ginny's cabin is hard beneath me, and I shift slightly to get more comfortable. It's a beautiful day, warm, slight breeze, birds chirping. The view from their front door is breathtaking. An open space that flows into pines and aspens that flank a distant mountain range, covered in snow. They chose the perfect spot to build their home.

I'll remain here for as long as needed to make sure Ginny's all right.

Ginny. The thought of holding her in my arms at Jake's funeral plays in my mind. I close my eyes and sigh. Yes, I can still feel her against my chest. If only it were under different circumstances. She held on to me, but her desire was for another. Her husband.

I rip my hat off and shove my fingers through my hair. What

kind of a man am I to be wantin' a dead man's wife? Hopping from the step, I pace in front of the cabin. Regardless, I'll be here for her. She's all alone and she'll need protection.

From the moment she and Jake arrived at our camp, I haven't been able to take my eyes off her. Every day I think about how lucky Jake is to have her. How lucky he *was* to have her. Her face glows when she smiles. Her eyes twinkle. I sigh. So many times I've imagined what it'd be like to slide my fingers through her hair or wrap my arms around her tiny little waist, or Lord help me, feel those voluptuous breasts in the palms of my hands. Taking her in my arms the way I see Jake do so often. The love they share is never hidden.

To her, I'm only one of the fellas, a miner. Dirty, smelly, hairy. She doesn't care about me. I'm the last thought on her mind. I know it's a terrible thing, imagining that maybe there might be a chance for me and her now. Jake's body is practically still warm and I'm thinking about how I yearn to take his wife as my own. At the same time, I miss my friend. Jake is…was a good man.

I'll never forget the night they first arrived at our camp, and when I first laid eyes on Ginny.

My stomach grumbles as I slop up beans with a hunk of bread, when a voice calls out of the dark, the face of a young man appears in the light of the fire.

"Excuse me. I hear there might be work to be had at this camp?"

Everyone goes silent. Lee takes his fiddle from his arm to rest in his lap.

The young man steps forward, closer to our circle. "I was in Sutton's Creek and a gentleman by the name of Mister Riley said I could find work here. Are one of you the foreman?"

"Who's askin'?" Old Man Marshall speaks up, his voice gruff, as though he weren't a weak old drunk.

I chuckle to myself, shake my head, and dig back into my beans.

"Jake. Jake Price. And this is my wife."

I peer up to see this Jake fellow reach into the dark and pull the hand of the most beautiful woman I've ever seen into the light. She tucks a stray blonde lock behind her ear and blushes as she steps forward. We all get to our feet quicker than a calvary scout's charge.

Marshall tips his hat. "Ma'am."

"Please, call me Ginny," her voice is like silk against my ears.

From that moment on, she's had a special place in my heart and mind. Now here I am, a slimy son-of-a-bitch, hanging around her stoop, still wanting her to be mine.

This isn't really a place to bring your lovely young bride. But Jake had, knowing the high stakes. Ginny's always known too. As it turns out, she's one tough woman. This mountain has roughened her up a bit, but not so much to weather her beautiful smile or spirit. When Jake asked that I take care of Ginny if anything were to ever happen to him, I said of course, not thinking anything ever truly would. We'd had bad injuries in the camp, broken limbs, ribs, collar bones. We've had falls and even a stabbing once. Damn Tucker fell on his own knife while enjoying too much moonshine. I chuckle and shake my head at the memory. But Jake's the first in our camp to die since I've been here.

Oh, Jake. He'd do anything for anybody. Such a kind man who had no fear of nothin'. A breath of new life. And full of childhood shenanigans. His love for Ginny extended beyond this hardened world. He spoke of her every day with his face alight like the doggone sun. He was going to build her a proper house and they were going to have a gaggle of little ones running around.

I promised you I'd care for her, Jake, and I intend to keep that promise. I know we never discussed the extent of me caring for her, but I hope you'll be all right with me making her mine. If she's in agreement, of course.

I'm unsure that's something she could ever agree to. Although, she might have to. I let out a long breath and hang my head. For now, I'll let her get some rest. Tomorrow's a new day.

3

Ginny

It's been two weeks since we buried Jake. The men are so kind to bring me food even though I don't care to eat. Truth is, I don't wish to see or speak to anyone. I know they mean well, but I do wish they'd let me be.

As I curl up on my bed, my dress feels enormous, almost like a blanket draped around me, and I can't help but think I should probably take it in. Who cares how I look. I have no one to pretty myself up for anymore. Wiping away another tear from my sore puffy eyes, I decide to lay here until I die. I'd hate for the men to find me like this, especially Joe. He has been most protective and concerned about me. But I can't go on. I can't get up. Hollowness fills me. I'm. Just. So. Empty.

The rain hits the roof in a steady, gentle flow. I'm glad for the gray skies, because I can't bear to see the sun shine one more day. If I'm lucky, I'll die before it dares to show its cheery face again.

I close my eyes and melt further into the grass filled mattress knowing Jake will never again lay beside me or hold me.

A strange sound nudges me up to listen. I sit still waiting to hear it again. A whimper? I haven't seen a child in the camp except for the few families who passed through in the spring. There it is again. Leaning forward, I hope to fully hear it better. Something is jiggling on the door. When I step from the bed my knees almost collapse. I'm weaker than I knew. Slowly I open the door to peer out when a soaked pup, a beagle, looks up as if asking to come in.

"Well, hello," I say, coaxing it inside. "What are you doing in this weather?"

It rubs its wet shivering body against my leg the way Mother's cat would do.

"Let's get you dry." I grab a blanket, sit on the floor, take him into my lap, and cuddle him. "My guess is that you're hungry too." But he closes his eyes and falls asleep in my arms. His presence feels familiar, but I don't know this pup. Why do I have this overwhelming sense that Jake has sent him to get me out of bed?

I know if Jake were here, he'd have told me days ago I needed to, "get up and keep living." Living isn't something I wish to do anymore. Surely the dog deserves to exist though, so I slowly take him from my lap, nestled in the blanket, to the floor. I light a lamp before I move to the cold stove to make him and myself something to eat. Thankfully Joe brought wood in yesterday. He said it looked like a storm was on the horizon and wanted to be sure I had dry logs. He stoked the fire and urged me to eat, then left with a huff when I didn't respond. Since I haven't moved from the bed I'd let the fire die, like my insides.

As I stir the stew, I feel so strongly that Jake is standing behind me that I turn faster than you can bat an eye. "Jake!" But he's not there. That can't be. I felt him behind me. My eyes dart around the room. No. No Jake. I hang my head. It's the little dog, sitting at my feet, staring up at me now with his head cocked to the side.

Bending down, I extend my hand. He inches closer, nuzzling his head in my palm. "Jake did send you, didn't he?" I find myself smiling for the first time since losing my husband. It's true, he's not dead. He just doesn't live in his earthly body anymore. There's that knowing again I can't explain. A knowing in this very moment that he's still with me, but in a different way. And there's a knowing that this sweet animal needs me. Perhaps I need him too.

4

Silas

1866 (January, three years earlier) Ireland

My heart thumps wildly as the men shout and cheer against the ropes of the ring. They call out my name, giving the rush I need to win this fight. I open and close my bloody fists. The scent of sweat and body odor mingle with the coppery smell of the crimson liquid that runs from my nose. Hopefully it's not broken.

Solving life's challenges with my hands began as a way to survive, but once the element of financial reward was introduced, it became an addiction. Since moving to my father's homeland, I learned quickly that I could make more in one boxing brawl than I could working ten to twelve hours a day digging trenches and laying stones for an entire month. My father raised me to be an excellent stone mason, but life has made me an even better fighter.

These scoundrels who shout encouragements to me and throw money in the hat, they worship me. They wish they were me, and the women, they practically beg to be with me. They all wish to bed down with the American prize fighter who is good with his hands in more ways than one.

"Go on, get him, lad!"

A shout from the edge of the ring snaps me back to reality just as a punch connects with my jaw, sending my bloody shrapnel across the dirty makeshift mat. I lose my balance and stumble back into the ropes.

I spit and shake sense back into my head. I'm tired—tired of fighting and running away and tired of this life I've made for myself here in Ireland. The land is beautiful, and the people have been welcoming, but it's not my land, nor are they my people, despite my father's family originating from here.

Tucking my right arm in to protect my stomach and leaving my left arm extended to keep my opponent at a distance, my feet work as if in a choreographed dance while the man swings his bare knuckles at me. I've done this enough to know he's wearing himself out. Sweat runs down his cheeks from his soaked hair and his glazed eyes droop. His feet waiver as he swings wildly at my face, and I flinch back just in time to miss a punch to the side of my head. Hitting my skull will hurt him more than it hurts me. He provides me with a perfect shot of his torso. My right arm unfurls and lands a hard blow into his gut, soft for me, the end for him.

Stephen slaps a satchel full of money into my bruised hand. "I'll see ya next week, my friend."

I nod, not ready to tell him I plan to go back home to America. He's been my closest and longest friend while living here, so I must speak with him about it. I'll tell him, but not now. Tonight isn't the time.

"Stephen, would you meet me at the Seaside Inn on Tuesday morning for a cuppa?"

Stephen tilts his head. "Is everythin' grand?"

The relief of my decision lifts and I give a shaky laugh. "Yes, everything is all right."

"I'll see ya Tuesday then." He pats my arm, and I step out onto the sidewalk.

White clouds form around my face with every exhale in this frosty January air. I pull my coat tighter around my neck and tuck my head down.

From my periphery, I see Peggy push off the brick wall of the building while placing the cap back on her flask. "I've been waitin' on ya."

"It's cold out here. You should be home where it's warm."

She runs her hand over my collar and shoves the flask into my chest. "I've been waitin' for ye to keep me warm."

I take a swig of the whiskey and slip it into the pocket of her coat while studying her. Her auburn hair flows from her hat and down her shoulders. It's tempting to bring her to my cottage tonight, one last tryst. She and Stephen have been my constant since I stepped off the boat a little over three years ago. Right away, I began working for her father, Peter Burke, a tyrant of a man.

Thankfully, I met Stephen within a week, and he introduced me to "an easy way to make money." Bareknuckle prize fighting.

As it turned out, I'm a natural at it. But then again, it's always been my way of life.

I've considered from time-to-time marrying Peggy for the sole purpose of getting her out of her father's house, but that wouldn't be fair to her or me. We don't love each other.

I take one of her red curls in my hand allowing it to twist around my finger. "I'm going home, Peg."

She wraps her arms around my waist and giggles. "Aye. I'm comin' with ye."

Stepping back, I take her arms and place them at her sides. "No. I'm going home to America."

Her brows furrow. "What do ya mean goin' home to America?"

"I no longer wish to live this life of fighting for a living." I point to my battered face.

"But that's what ye are, a fighter." She crosses her arms over her chest.

I shove my hands in my pockets. "Only for survival. I no longer wish to survive, but to live. I miss home."

Peggy taps her foot. "So, yer a quitter then." She says it as a statement, but her brows rise in question.

"No. I'm not a quitter." I don't feel like having this conversation with her now, out here in the cold night. My body is sore and exhausted. I know she doesn't truly care about me, but rather her status of being associated with a champion. There were others before me and there will be others after me.

Her lips form into a thin line. "Fine then. Have yerself a good time in America."

Her attitude makes me smirk. "Goodbye, Margaret Burke." I step towards her and wrap my arms around her shoulders. She looks away standing stock still. I breathe in the peppermint scent of her hair. She's tough on the outside but I know inside she's as soft as my ma's mashed potatoes.

Peggy shakes her head, swiping away a tear. "I won't miss ya."

I smile. "I know."

She softens and returns my hug. "Goodbye, Silas Flynn. And may the road rise up to meet ye. May the wind be always at yer back. May the sun shine warm upon yer face; the rains fall soft upon yer fields." Taking the flask from her pocket, she slips it into mine. "And until we meet again, may God hold ye in the palm of His hand." She sniffles and walks away.

Although it feels wonderful to be off the boat and back on American soil, the urgency to get to wide open spaces gnaws at me. Manhattan is much too crowded for this country boy. People of every race and nationality are bustling about. The streets are narrow and dusty with the clomping of horses and wagons. Tall brick buildings line the roadways. Vendors litter the sidewalks selling their wares—baked goods, tobacco, clothing, and household items.

A Newsboy runs back and forth waving a paper. "The war's over," he shouts. "Read all about it. General Lee's surrendered."

A hope stirs in me as I navigate through the throng to get to the child.

I nod towards the boy's paper. "How much?"

"Five cents, sir."

I set my travel bag down, dig in my pocket, and pull out ten cents. "Keep it."

His eyes widen. "Land sakes. Thanks, Mister."

Sure enough, the front page of the New York Times reads, "Union, Victory! Peace! Surrender of General Lee and His Whole Army." A victory indeed.

I can't predict what life will be like in this new America, but as I lay on the boat, overwhelmed by seasickness and feeling like I was dying, I made a promise to myself: when I set foot back on solid ground, I would start living my life the right way. No more fighting. No more women. But first, I must find the nearest hotel and restaurant and regain my land legs.

5

Ginny

1869 Sutton's Creek, Colorado Territory

The crackle of campfire and the scent of whiskey relaxes my weary muscles. That aching in the pit of my stomach that Jake is never coming back still lingers. After six months, I wonder if it'll ever go away. Old Man Marshall says time will lessen it. I sure hope he's right. I know drinking only intensifies it, but I can't help but partake in the liquor as it's passed around.

The ache grows stronger at the thought of telling these men I must go back to New York. Oh, how I'll miss them. How I'll miss these mountains and the memories I have here with Jake. I can't help but feel like I'm betraying our dream somehow by leaving. Our dream of living in the West. Giving up our claim will be hard to do. And Jake's body rests here, just over yonder near the tree's edge beneath a pile of stones I placed myself. I won't be able to visit, which I planned to do eventually, telling him about our new little beagle, Buck. Or how the men invite me to eat with them, so I don't have to cook. How they include me in their nightly campfire ritual of singing, playing instruments, and passing the bottle.

They do their best to be respectful of the fact that I'm a lady, but I'm no prude and have insisted they treat me like one of the men. I'll miss them so.

I take another swig as the bottle reaches me, swallowing down the liquid courage. Maybe they won't care. Perhaps I'm a burden on them. It's a thought I hadn't considered until now. They've been caring for me for months. Months. Somehow it doesn't feel like months since Jake died. It feels like it's been mere weeks.

Standing with all the confidence I can muster I raise my voice, "Gentlemen, may I have your attention?"

Silence falls around the fire. My body feels light as I stare into their serious faces which causes a nervous giggle to escape me. My skirt is balled into my hands and quickly I speak the words. "I'm going back to New York."

The fire crackles and pops as eyeballs peer back at me.

"I can't stay here," I continue, now wringing my hands. "The notion that I could do this on my own is ridiculous." I chuckle and wipe away a tear that's sliding down my face, wishing someone will say something.

As if reading my thoughts, Lee clears his throat. "We'll miss you all right, Ginny, but if you think going back is what's best, then we understand." He looks around. "Don't we boys?"

There are some grunts and shifting of feet and bodies.

"I reckon."

"Yes."

"Whatever you think best."

I hear and feel disappointment and my heart is heavy.

"You fellas don't need a woman hanging around," I chuckle. "I hate being a burden to you. There's nothing left here for me, and I can't do this on my own." I glance at each one of them, their faces downcast.

Old Man Marshall shuffles over and puts an arm around me. I inhale the scent of earth, body odor, and liquor. "You're like a daughter to some of us. A sister to others. We'll miss you something awful, but we understand." He holds out his hand. "Joe, hand me that bottle. We're going to celebrate Ginny."

"To Ginny!" they shout in unison, and my heart lightens. I sure love these men. They've been my rock since Jake died. Especially Joe. I can't imagine my life without them. But I couldn't imagine my life without Jake either and yet here I am, living without him.

I'm unsteady on my feet after all the dancing and drinking we've done.

"Woah," says Lee as he grabs me by the arm to keep me from tumbling into the fire.

"I'll walk her home." Big Joe steps up and gives me his arm.

I've never had to walk home in the dark alone because I'm theirs and they protect me. It brings me comfort.

"They're bears, mountain lions, and worse—heathens—out there." Old Man Marshall once told me. The fellas watch over me like a mother hen, or dare I say, a mother bear.

"Thank you, Joe." I take his elbow with both hands. "Come on, Buck." The little dog jumps to his feet from his warm spot near the flames.

"Goodnight, Ginny," call the men.

It's a chilly night, as most Colorado mountain nights are. The stars twinkle above us through the trees, and I think of how small we are.

"Do you believe there's truly a heaven?" I say, breaking the silence between me and Joe.

Twigs and gravel crunch under our feet.

"I try not to think about it."

"I don't believe it's real."

Joe pats my hands that still hold his arm. "I believe you've had a bit too much to drink."

There's a smile in his words. He's probably right.

"Thank you for walking me home," I say as we reach my front steps.

"Let's get your lantern lit," he insists. "I want to make sure you can see all right before I leave. I better stoke the fire too."

"Oh, that's not necessary, Joe, I can take care of it." I swat his arm feeling the effects of the whiskey and lift the latch on the cabin door. "I'll be all right, you don't have to worry about me anymore."

"No, I insist." He makes his way in and finding the matches on the table, lights the oil lamp.

"Ginny." His voice wavers.

"What is it, Joe?"

He shakes the match sending a whisp of smoke curling in the air as he replaces the glass chimney over the flame of the light. "May I sit?"

"Of course." I take a seat near him at the crude table. The one Jake fashioned himself after we built the cabin.

Joe taps his fingers on the wood and glances about. His dark curls hang slightly over his eyes. I've never thought about his looks before besides how big and strong he is. In fact, he appears almost too large to be sitting at this table. His face is youthful, but the lines around his eyes tell a story of a life lived hard. He's never spoken of his life before coming to the camp, and I never pried. The men who wish to tell you their stories will.

"I've been thinking, Ginny." He swipes his fingers over his mustache and down his beard. Then he taps the table again. Clearly something is heavy on his mind.

I chuckle. "Well, what is it, Joe?"

He reaches over and places a large hand over both of mine that are folded in front of me. Leaning in, I'm anticipating his words. I glance down at his hand on mine then back to his face. His eyes are blue and his lashes dark. How have I never noticed his eyes before? There's sadness there.

"I know it hasn't been that long since…" He looks down then back up at me before clearing his throat. "Since, Jake." His Adam's apple bobs. My hands sweat beneath his palm. "I know it hasn't been that long," he repeats. "But I'd like to take care of you, Ginny."

The flame in the lantern flickers.

"You have been taking great care of me, Joe. I can't imagine anyone doing a more favorable job and I thank you." I give him a genuine smile. He's such a sweet man.

He frowns. "I know you don't want to go back to New York, and I hate seeing you all alone. I'd be right good to you; I believe you know that."

I remove my hands and wipe them on my skirt. Buck sleeps soundly on the floor. He's such a lazy dog. *I'd be right good to you.* Joe's words echo in my mind. He wishes for more. He wishes to be my man.

"Ginny, please say something. Tell me to get the hell out. Just say something."

There's a stirring in me. I don't know where it's come from. Perhaps the liquor, but I can't seem to control it. My breaths grow shallow and a heat washes over my body.

Buck snores softly from his spot near the stove.

Joe wishes for me to be his. The realization of his words reverberates. It's been so long since I've been touched, and the knowing alone that he desires me has ignited something I can't seem to control.

Slowly I lean into him, placing my hand on the back of his head, and kiss his lips. He's hesitant at first, unsure if this is truly what I want, but then he reaches for me and draws me over to sit upon his knee. Cupping my face, he softly reciprocates my kiss. Pressing harder, my tongue reaches further into his mouth. The fire in me burns brighter as my lips move to his neck, and I unbutton the top of his shirt.

"Oh, Ginny," he whispers through bated breaths.

Joe lifts me and places me on the bed mere feet away. I don't know what I'm doing or why, but I can't bring myself to stop. There's a primal need within me to have this man, despite the unfamiliarity of his mouth, his touch, and his scent. I don't know what to do with this or how to feel about it. *It's all right,* I tell myself. He'll become familiar in time.

He shimmies from his suspenders and unbuttons the rest of his shirt.

An owl's faint call echoes in the distance.

I smooth my hands over Joe's foreign but solid chest and arms. I've never been with a man other than Jake. This is so new. A part of me is screaming to stop. I'm being unfaithful to my husband. Another part of me longs to be touched, to be loved. I've been so lonely.

His chest is warm against my lips as I trail light pecks across it, traveling up to his neck.

The golden light dances across the ceiling of the room, making his tanned face appear even darker. I'm reminded that his fragrance is foreign as I inhale his beard. My face burrows in his earthy scented hair as he lays light kisses on my bare shoulder.

His mouth makes its way to my breasts while reaching between my legs and up my skirt. A soft moan escapes my lips as his large fingers slide over the wetness through my pantalettes. I haven't been touched in so long, and I need this. I've yearned for Jake's body against mine. But Jake's not here, so Joe must do. I'm not ashamed. A defiance builds in me at the injustice of the situation.

The fire crackles in the stove as Joes slides my skirt down and tosses it on the floor.

No words are spoken between us, only heavy breaths and deep moans. He unbuttons his trousers, and I reach in drawing his girth out into my hand. He's large. Much larger than Jake.

Jake doesn't leave my thoughts as Joe pulls my pantalettes down, leaving me bare, and dropping them on the floor with the rest of our garments. Fondling my nipple with the tip of his tongue, he opens my legs, wedging himself between them.

Jake. Oh, Jake. My body betrays me as liquid soaks my depths. *No, I mustn't do this. I can't.* Tears cloud my eyes, and I gently push Joe away while moving back. "Stop. Please stop."

"Ginny?" His brows furrow.

I grab the blankets and pull them over my naked body. "I can't do this Joe. I'm sorry. I thought I could, but I'm not ready."

Sadness fills his eyes as he slinks back. "I can't say I'm not disappointed, but I understand." He takes his drawers from the floor and puts them on, tucking his hard shaft inside.

There's an ache in my chest as I watch him dress and tears continue to cloud my vision.

"However long you need, Ginny, I'll be here."

"You'd wait for me?" I ask, unable to comprehend his words.

He sits on the side of my bed and runs the back of his finger over my cheek. "I've waited this long."

I wish to know what he means when he says he's waited this long. My mouth opens then closes.

The bed creaks as he reaches for his boots, and I take his arm. "Joe?"

His eyes are tender, and there's a twinge in my chest as I watch him.

"Thank you."

He nods and slips his shoes on. "Good night, Ginny."

I close my eyes as he leans in, leaving a soft kiss upon my head. "Make sure you lock the door behind me," he whispers.

I nod and he tilts my chin, placing another kiss upon my lips.

A battle rages within me, torn between urging him to stay and letting him go.

When the door closes behind him, I allow the tears to fall.

6

Joe

Waking up this morning recalling the feel of Ginny's bare body is the best way to start the day. It's the best thing that can happen to a guy like me way up here in these unforgiving mountains. Sure, I go into Sutton's Creek every now and then with the fellas to visit Clansy Mae's Finest, but those ladies have nothing on Virginia Price. She's fun and beautiful, and damn she can kiss. I know she needs more time and I'm all right with that. She'll come around before I even realize it.

"Where's your head at, Joe? If you're not careful, you're going to smash your thumb." Lee's shadow hovers over me. My thoughts aren't on the spike I'm hammering but on how good it felt to have my lips on a naked Ginny last night.

The image of her breasts in my mouth plays repeatedly in my mind. Her passionate kisses as if she's been starving for me causes me to grow hard and I shake my head and focus on the spike to quell my *rising* excitement. I'll have her back in my arms soon enough.

I'm unsure if it would be right for us to live in the cabin she and Jake built together. Although, it only makes sense since it's already built and it's a good solid home. And now that she has me, she doesn't have to go back to New York. There's a reason for her to stay. Me, I'm the reason.

Whistling a cheerful melody, I put all my strength into hammering down on the spike before me.

I can imagine a handful of children running around shouting, "Mama," and Ginny having that big bright smile on her face at what we've created together. I wonder if they'll have curly hair like mine or straight like hers. Will they be blonde like their mama or dark haired like me?

"What are you smiling about?"

I stop hammering and look up at Tucker, realizing I'm grinning so big my face aches a little. "It's a beautiful day that's all, Tuck. Can't you see the sun's shining, and can't you feel the warmth on your face?" I turn towards the glaring heat and smile wider. "The birds are singing."

"You got yourself a special someone, Joe? Does one of Clancy Mae's girls got you all poetic today? You best be careful. Those ladies aren't the kind you fall in love with."

I look down at the piece of metal I've been pounding on and feel a flutter in my stomach, anticipating seeing Ginny again tonight after a long day of working. "It's just a beautiful day, Tucker."

Deciding I can't wait until after supper to see Ginny, I make my way to her cabin—dirty, dusty and all. As I approach her steps, a blood curdling scream causes my feet to move faster than they ever have. *It's Ginny. Oh God!* I can't help imagining that she's being mauled by a bear or a mountain lion. Nearing the screams, I come to a halt at the sight of her sprawled across Jake's grave, wailing in pain. Not a physical pain, but a brokenhearted pain.

I steady my breaths, weighing whether I should go comfort her. Then I hear her cries. "I promise, I'll never do such a shameful thing again, and I'll never replace you, Jake. I love you."

Knowing she's referring to her and me, what we did, my throat tightens and my chin trembles. My feet falter as I reach out for the tree beside me. I remove my hat and hold my head. The pain that grips my heart is almost more than I can bear.

7

Ginny

I haven't been able to bring myself to visit Jake's grave since he died, but today I'm going.

As I approach the mound of stones, nausea overtakes me. I feel like a little girl afraid to tell my mother I've broken something important in fear of punishment. It's only a pile of rocks, I remind myself. Besides, I know I don't have to come here to visit Jake. He knows what I've done. The shameful thing I've done. I swallow back the disgust and cover my mouth with my hands. Slowly I bend, reaching out to touch the cold stones. It doesn't feel real that he's in there, that his body is under this debris. It's as though I'm lifting out of my own flesh and hovering above my body.

"Oh, Jake." The tears come uncontrollably. "I'm so sorry. I'm so terribly sorry." I lay across the cold stones and weep. "I've been unfaithful to you and I'm so ashamed. I'm so ashamed. I don't even recognize myself. I loathe myself for what I've done. Can you ever forgive me? Please forgive me. Please." There's a pounding in my head and the need to vomit takes over, only I swallow it back then wail my apologies, my pleas for forgiveness, into the crevices of the rocks.

"I promise, I'll never do such a shameful thing again, and I'll never replace you, Jake. I love you."

For the first time since he passed, I'm able to truly let go of all the emotions I've been holding on to. Crying, screaming, pounding on the earth, this is what I've needed to move it through and out of me.

When I've cried and howled until I have no tears left to shed, and my voice can barely make a sound, I lay still. Silent. Sprawled out on the mound as if I'm hugging Jake. I can't leave him. I'll never leave him. No one will ever be a substitute for him. Ever.

I wake to Buck whimpering with his little paws against the rocks. Realizing that exhaustion had taken over and I'd drifted off to sleep, I push myself up from where I lay, promising Jake I'll return tomorrow to visit him. I'll visit him every day for the rest of my life.

Although there's a heaviness in me from all the crying, my soul feels lighter.

I take Buck into my arms and hug him to me. "It's okay, boy," I lay a gentle smooch on his head and place him back to the ground.

A smile comes to my puffy face as the sun softly kisses it. I imagine Jake laying feathery sweeps of his lips across my cheek and down the slope of my nose. Everything's all right. He and I are starting over, even though not physically together, we're still as one spiritually.

"Come on, Buck. Let's fetch a bucket so we can pick berries and make the fellas a pie for dinner this evening." I exhale a long sigh of contentment as I make my way to the cabin with the little dog in tow.

I'm unsure of how I'm going to speak with Joe tonight, but it's a conversation we must have. I know he'll be heartbroken as he has his sights set on us marrying but in my heart, I'm married to Jake. Oh, I know the Bible says we're no longer bound, but Jake's death has changed my mind about what that book tells us. Jake's still my husband, and that's that. Until death does us part now means *my* death.

I hesitate before leaving my front steps. Everything is different now and I'm unsure how I'll face Joe. But I'm resolved to not allow this to go on. I take a deep breath and slip my shawl over my shoulders before heading up to camp.

A relief washes over me when I don't see Joe. "I brought biscuits and a wild berry pie, fellas." I set the basket and tin on a makeshift table that holds other dinner items. There's an animal, rabbit it appears, I don't pay much attention, roasting over the fire. "It sure smells good." I smile nervously wondering if they know what Joe and I almost did last night. What we *did* do. I feel like that guilty girl who came home to face Mother after losing my virginity to Jake in his family's hay loft. I feared she'd see it in my eyes, on my face, hear it in my voice, or smell it on me. Thank goodness she didn't suspect a thing.

Old Man Marshall hands me a bottle of moonshine as I sit beside him.

"Oh, I better not tonight." Concerned that it may impair my judgement and send me back to the arms of Joe despite my promise to Jake, I've decided against drinking this evening.

"That doesn't sound like the Ginny I know." He furrows his brows. "But suit yourself." He takes a swig and passes it on.

Tucker clears his throat. "We fellas have been thinking, Ginny. We don't want you to go. We know how much you love it here, so we got a proposal of sorts."

I glance around at the smiling faces that bring a grin to mine. "What is it?" I ask. "Although I can't be marrying all of ya."

They laugh, and Tucker continues. "In case you haven't noticed, we're not the cleanest out here in these hills."

"I'm not sure what that has to do with me, but go on."

"We'd like to pay you to wash our clothes. Your own laundress business of sorts. And we'll send business your way when we can from outside the camp."

"Laundress business?" I don't quite understand.

"It's not glamorous, we know," says Lee. "But it's the only way we can think of to help you stay. An incentive if you will." He shoves the toe of his boot into the dirt. "We don't want you to go, Ginny. We love you. And we'd sure miss your biscuits."

I laugh and lean into Old Man Marshall, who sits beside me staring into the fire with watery eyes. "That's some proposal."

My heart sings with delight that they're wishing to help me. Fact is, they've been helping since Jake died. "Can I think about it?" I glance around at the faces staring back at me.

"Sure, you can," says Tucker. "But don't think too long because I've got a pair of under drawers that can practically stand up by themselves, they're so dirty."

Laughter fills the air as sparks from the fire dance off into the starry night sky.

"Goddamn, Tucker, we don't need to know that." Lee takes the rabbit from the flames shaking his head.

Sitting on a stump with a tin plate of food on my lap I can't help but notice Joe still hasn't come to dinner. I clear my throat and lean towards Marsh. "Where's Big Joe?"

"Oh, he left camp today." He looks at me wide eyed. "He didn't go tell you?"

My heart sinks and my head swirls with confusion. "No." I'm staring at Marsh, my fork suspended in the air. *What does he mean Joe left camp?*

"He said it was high time he moved on and sought another mine." Marsh scoops his beans with his biscuit. "Said there was nothin' to keep him here. I can't believe he didn't see you before going." He wags his head.

My stomach plunges and I've lost all appetite for the food on my plate. I don't know what to say or think. Perhaps I should be relieved. But I thought he wished to marry me. Perhaps that was a deception to get in my bed. I see, when I say no to him, he up and leaves. I suppose I should be more ashamed for how far we did get, but I'm not. I'm angry. How dare he. But, if I'm honest with myself, I'm no better.

I sit my tin plate aside. "Fellas, it's been a long day. I believe I'll call it a night. Be sure to eat up that pie and those biscuits. I don't want any leftovers."

"No need to worry about that." Lee holds up a piece of bread before shoving it into his mouth.

"Come, Buck." I snap my fingers and step away from the fire.

"Hold up there, Ginny," Tucker shouts.

He sits his plate down and wipes his mouth with his sleeve. "I'll walk you home."

"That's all right, Tucker. I'm a grown woman."

"No, I insist," he says, catching up to me. "'Sides," he states in a low tone. "Joe asked me to give you this." He reaches in his pocket and pulls out a letter with a wax seal.

Warmth rushes over my face and neck. What does Tucker know? Does he know what me and Joe did? "Tucker, I—" I begin to make an excuse. Tell him we didn't go all the way, or something along those lines. But he cuts me off.

"I suppose he felt bad for not getting a chance to tell you goodbye, so he preferred to tell you in a letter." Tucker winks. "You were like a sister to him. I know he was always frettin' over you." He shrugs. "For whatever reason, he asked me not to give it to you in front of the fellas."

I clutch the missive to my chest. "Thank you."

Once Tucker has seen to it that I'm safe inside my cabin, we wish each other a good night and I run to the lamp light opening the seal of the letter as quickly as I can.

Dear Ginny,

I sit in the chair to steady myself. Holding my breath, I read.

You must think me a coward to not tell you goodbye in person, but I can't bear to see you. I know I'd want you too bad and I know I can't have you, not the way I'd like, or need.

I saw you today, at Jake's gravesite. I heard screams and set off running thinking maybe a bear had you, but it was pain that had you all torn up. You still belong to Jake in your heart. I knew it when you were in my arms, but I didn't allow myself to believe it. Now I know for certain you can never be mine. It's not fair to you or me. I won't cause you anymore pain, so I'm leaving. It's for the best. Seeing you and not being able to have you may be too much for my heart to bear.

I'll always remember you.

Take care, Ginny.

Joe

8

Ginny

I'm unsure where my head was when I considered going back to New York, but that is no longer a thought. I won't have my mother snubbing her nose at me with the reminder I never should have left. I can almost hear her voice, already preparing to say the words that she would inevitably speak, *"Jake's death is all your fault."* No, I'm staying on this mountain, in the home Jake and I built together. I shall breathe my last right here.

It's a beautiful sunny day, so I take the men's clothing outside with my wash bucket and get to work in the shade of the maple tree. Buck rests beside me and I take a moment to watch his little body move with every breath and exhale. Oh, to have no cares in the world. It must be nice. I shake my head and grab a grimy shirt from the laundry pile.

As I push the soiled garment into the water, the heat scorches my hands, but I have grown accustomed to the burn.

A whiff of Rocky Mountain Columbine greets my nose, giving me a reason to smile, when a shadow suddenly falls over me. Two men, strangers, stand above me. One is a spindly fellow with a weathered face and the other has crooked teeth that show through the abundant hair covering his face.

"Ma'am." The scrawny one tips his hat to me.

My scalp prickles.

"You gentlemen have clothing you need laundered?" I peer up from under the rim of my hat.

They appear much older than me and their clothes are filthy. The toe of the skinny man's boot is coming apart at the seam.

"Where's your husband?" The man with crooked teeth glances around scratching at his beard.

My mouth is suddenly pasty and I'm figuring how I can get past them and into the house. "Do you need something?" Holding the washboard tightly I stand.

"We need to speak with your husband," scrawny spits.

"About?" I step back.

Buck is awake and at my side.

"Well, that's for menfolk." He turns to crooked teeth and laughs.

"My husband and I discuss everything." I square my shoulders, not letting them sense any fear in me.

Crooked teeth glides his eyes up and down my body. "Truth is, you ain't got no husband...do you?"

"I certainly do. His name is Jake Price."

"*Was* named Jake Price." He inches closer.

"What business do you have here?" I take another step back. Buck's growling now as he too knows something isn't right with these fellows.

Scrawny does a little dance around me and Buck. "I'll shoot him like I did your man if you don't shut him up, *little miss widow*."

My body tenses and I grip the washboard harder. Joe reassured me he'd killed the man who took Jake's life, and a knowing tells me this man is lying to scare me.

"Buck, it's okay, boy," I say in my sweetest voice.

A breeze sweeps over the droplets of sweat on my neck.

"Yeah, that's it, good boy, Buck." Crooked teeth cackles.

Scrawny grabs my arms from behind, causing me to drop the board, while crooked teeth lunges. He kicks Buck. A yelp rings out and I scream as crooked teeth tears open my shirt. My hat falls from my head as scrawny places his filthy hand over my mouth. A combination of shit and tobacco makes me want to retch.

"Oh, those are big and round." Staring at my bare chest, crooked tooth licks his lips. "You're going to play wife with us today, you hear?" He continues to leer at my breasts while pulling his suspenders from his shoulders.

Buck's barking again, and although the men are paying him no mind, the sound is deafening to me. My body trembles uncontrollably and my vision becomes a blur.

"Hurry up, Clarence," says scrawny. "I want my turn. Her tits got me hard as a stump." His face rests against mine as he peers over my shoulder. I turn my head at the putrid smell that emerges from his mouth as he breathes so close to my nose.

"Don't worry, Bill, you'll get your chance right quick here. It'll only take me a second," says the man I now know as

Clarence. He's salivating as he glares at my breasts and lifts my skirt. "Oh, yeah," he moans, running his hand between my legs.

I close my eyes. My heart beats wildly and the warm sensation of piss runs down my legs and into my boots. Buck's barking seems miles away as all I hear is the sound of my own heartbeat.

"Shut that damn dog up. I swear I'll shoot him." Bill moves his grimy hand from my face.

I scream again and thrash fighting to free myself as Clarence struggles to pull down my urine soaked pantalettes.

"Hold her still, damnit," Clarence grits.

Bill brings his hand back to my mouth and nose, pinning me to his shoulder. "I'll break your neck if you move a muscle. Now be a good girl and this will all be over soon."

Just as Clarence pulls on my pantalettes, I tumble to the ground, limbs flailing. The other man, Bill, is laying behind me unconscious and Clarence is standing with his pants down and wide eyes that look past me.

I turn cautiously to see Old Man Marshall with a gun cocked and ready to fire. He must have used it to knock Bill out. I scramble to get up pulling on my drawers and my blouse. Gasping for air, I push back my hair that's now a disheveled mess.

"Get in the cabin, Ginny," Marsh thunders.

My mind tells me to obey, but my body won't move. Panting, I scan the ground around me. *I've lost something. What is it?*

"Now, Ginny."

My hat. Stumbling and tripping over my wash bucket I snatch it up. Buck's still barking. "Buck, come."

"Go, Ginny," Marsh shouts at me, sterner this time, and

I flinch. I've never heard him sound so severe. It's now that I notice he's holding two guns, one on each man.

My hands shake as I fall into the cabin and latch the door. I slide to the floor and sob. What would I have done had my friend not shown up? Those men were set on defiling me.

"Oh, Jake," I cry out into the room, curling my knees up, hugging them tight to my body. Burying my head into my skirt, I weep.

Two loud distinct pops of a gun ring out and Buck's barking ceases. *Buck!* He's not here with me. I scramble to my feet and look through the cracks in the door. Marsh walks up the hill with his hands resting on the guns at his sides while Buck sniffs at something on the ground. I open the door slightly and see the two men lying dead in the grass. The old man took the law into his own hands, just as Joe had when Jake was killed. There is no choice up here. That's why it's called the wild west.

I slide back down the door and the tears come in great waves.

A knock shakes me from the trance I've fallen into.

"Ginny, it's Lee. You in there?"

I open the door a crack to peek out. He must see the fright on my face. "It's all right now, those men are gone."

"Did Marsh have to kill them?" I ask.

Lee has one foot on a step leaning forward toward the door, his elbow rests on his knee. He glances about. "Ginny, you know when food is left out and the bears come time and time again to get more of it? Well, those men are like bears. They'd be back. You know as well as I do, they would, and next time might be worse."

Heat washes over me as if I had done something wrong. But I know, there's no reason for shame. They were wrong and Marsh protected me. Oh, Marsh. Now he has blood on his hands, because of me.

"Ginny, you got a gun?"

I nod, too afraid to speak in fear of bursting into tears. My eyes shift past Lee, scanning for anything or anyone who shouldn't be there.

"You're not to go anywhere without that gun, you hear me?" Lee orders.

I nod again.

"Do you know how to use it?"

I clear my throat. "Jake had me practice for when he was away from the house."

"Good. He was a good man, that Jake."

The lump in my throat grows at those words. Yes, he was a good man, and oh how I miss him more than ever right about now.

Buck finally bounds up to the door. I open it just enough to let him through. Still too sorry to look Lee in the eyes, I stare at his boot, dirty and worn. "Please thank Marsh for me." My voice lacks all confidence.

"There's no need. He was doing what any one of us would have done." He steps back onto the dusty ground. "But I'll tell him."

Out of my periphery I see he tips his hat to me and walks away.

"Oh, Ginny." He turns back. "We hope to see you for supper tonight. I'll send Tucker for you. If you decide not to join us, you let him know then."

I bow my head and shut the door. With both Jake and Joe gone, I know I must face this life for what it is, survival.

9

Silas

1872 (Present Day)

I stare out the window of my room onto the muddy Omaha, Nebraska soil. Mist lingers in the distance and a drizzle runs down the panes of glass. Although I made a promise to myself when returning from Ireland to live a better life, I've managed to do the opposite. Over the years, I've found myself moving from town to town with bloody knuckles and just enough money to get by until the next temporary job or illegal activity that pays. Now here I am, yet another town, making my way as far west as I can get.

Reverend George Brown, a rather large man whom I've had the misfortune of having to share a room with here at the boarding house, snaps his pocket watch. "You coming to dinner, Flynn?"

"I'll be right behind you."

As he leaves the room, I take my Bible from the bed and close my eyes. God, please help me to have a good attitude towards this man.

I met Reverend Brown on the rail ride out here, and although I found him to be loud and boastful, engaging with him softened my heart towards God's calling. Apparently, it's true that He works in mysterious ways. I found comfort in remembering the times my ma would read to me from her Bible. Stories of the gallant David against Goliath, and Samson who killed the Philistines and himself by pushing apart the pillars that held the temple. When the preacher's words turned to snores, I turned to my Bible—the one thing that, no matter the situation I have found myself in, has always been by my side.

Ma always wished for me to be a preacher. What a disappointment I must have been to her all these years. That's about to change.

"I'm starting seminary school soon, Ma," I whisper into the room. I only wish she were here so I could tell her. A letter shall have to do.

I set the book on the bedside table, wash my hands in the basin, and head to the dining room.

Missus Pratt serves the best food I've eaten in a long while. And clearly, Reverend Brown is enjoying it as well. The man is sucking fried chicken juice from his pudgy fingers.

"You say you're heading to the Territories?" Mister Thatcher directs his question to the reverend.

"Yes, sir," booms the man. "Gathering the Lord's flock and saving them all from the jaws of perdition. They're all nothing but a bunch of heathens, whores, and thieves out there." He snatches another slice of bread from the center of the table.

Mister Thatcher's eyes widen. "I see."

The reverend points to me. His lips are wet with grease and a deep sense of revulsion twists in my stomach. "When I went to the seminary school to give a good word for Mister Flynn here, I was told a church in the west needed a minister. They gave me this here letter." He pats his chest. "And told me to give it to the board when I arrive."

"And when do you leave?" There's an excitement in Mister Thatcher's tone. The same excitement I feel in my chest at the prospect of George Brown departing in the immediate future.

The table falls silent as the man drinks down his glass of milk, and we wait with bated breath for his response.

He smacks his lips and wipes them on the napkin tucked in the collar of his shirt. "I leave in three days' time."

Mister Thatcher scoops a fork of potatoes from his plate. "You don't say. Well, we'll miss you." He catches my eye before shoving the food into his mouth with a slight smirk.

I believe we'll all be relieved to see the man go.

Considering I'm not yet a preacher, and I don't begin seminary school for another two weeks, I decide to buy a bottle of whiskey and smuggle it back to my room. Missus Pratt is a Godfearing woman who made it clear she does not allow liquor in her boarding house. But I need something to help me through these next three days rooming with the blustery Reverend Brown.

The night air is warm enough that if it weren't for smuggling in a bottle of whiskey, I'd have left my coat behind. With my contraband hidden within the inside pocket, I approach the house. It's located on a tranquil street, so I'm surprised when I hear the faint crying of a young lady, but I keep walking because it's none of my business. A woman could be crying for any number of reasons. But then I hear that fat bastard's voice, so I stop to listen closer.

"Please, don't," she cries.

"You listen to me," says the reverend. "You can give me what I desire, or I can take it." Although it's dark, thanks to the moonlight I can see he has her pinned against the house with one hand while unbuttoning his trousers with the other.

"Please," the girl begs.

His breeches fall to his knees as he tears her blouse open.

"You said you were a preacher." She's attempting to reason with him.

"As a man of God, young lady, I have authority over you."

I grit my teeth, knowing there is no reasoning with this man.

He grabs her breast moving his head towards her neck just as I reach him. "Brown." I take his shoulder and swing him away from her.

He looks pathetic with his mouth agape and his drawers hanging down. "Mister Flynn." He stumbles as he attempts to pull at his clothing. "It's not how it looks." Pointing at the girl he continues his lie. "This woman is a temptress."

"You better go," I say to the girl, my eyes still on this

worthless man.

She sniffles. "I want to watch you hurt him."

"I'm not going to hurt him."

She closes her shirt over her breasts. "Watch out," she cries in a loud whisper.

I turn away from her just in time to see George Brown charging at me, a large rock raised high. I swing my left arm up to block the blow, then draw the whiskey bottle from my coat and crack it to the side of his head, sending him crumpling to the rain-soaked earth.

"I think someone's coming." The girl pulls at the back of my collar as I glare down at the man who lies limp in a heap of blood, glass, and muck. As I squat down to check the pulse of the dead man, a glint of white peeks out from the dark ground. I pluck it up, place it in my pocket, and grab the girl by the arm, running between the houses into the backyard.

Still holding her blouse closed she wipes her nose on her sleeve. "Thank you so much. You saved me."

"Do you live around here?" I whisper, pushing my fingers through my hair and straightening my coat.

She nods.

"Go on home and speak to no one about what happened. You hear me? No one."

A quiet sob escapes her lips as she nods again.

"All right, go on that way." I point in the opposite direction.

She obeys my command, and I remove my boots before quietly entering the dark kitchen of Missus Pratt's boarding house through the back door. Since I wasn't seen leaving, I'll slink back to my room, and no one shall be the wiser. While I believe my actions are justified, I'll seek God's forgiveness later. If this way of life wasn't behind me before, it is now.

50

10

Silas

Laurel Springs is a quaint town in the foothills of the Rocky Mountains. The businesses with their false fronts, some painted, some still rough sawn lumber, are beautiful against the hills with jagged outcroppings of rock and aspen trees.

At first glance, I don't see the church, but I do see an older looking gentleman lugging a coarse brown sack over his shoulder. Certainly he must live here and know how to direct me.

"Excuse me, sir, can you tell me which way to the Laurel Springs Church?" I ask bounding from the stagecoach.

"It's on the other end of town," he says. "I'm going back to my wagon. Follow me and I'll give you a ride."

"Why, that's very kind of you," I shift my bag from one hand to the other.

"That's what a good Christian does," he says matter-of-fact.

"Do you attend the Laurel Springs Church?"

"I do indeed. My wife, God rest her soul, and I raised our three young'ins in that church."

"You don't say. That's wonderful." I extend my hand. "The name's Silas Flynn. I'm the new preacher."

The man squints at my hand then peers at my face. "Yer kinda young to be a preacher, aren't you?"

"I don't believe God sets an age limit on spreading the gospel." My hand hangs in the air as the lanky man climbs into his wagon. I pull my hand back and study it a moment before joining him on the seat.

The tepid August morning suddenly feels much warmer. This may be one of the worst, of many, decisions of my life. Wondering how they will receive me, I realize I still don't know this gentleman's name.

Although in truth, the church is within walking distance of the stage station, I am grateful for the ride and thank the man for his kindness as I step from the wagon.

"You'll want to go to that there house." He points past the church to a home nestled in the trees. "That's where the McCalisters live. They'll see that you get settled in. See you Sunday." Snapping the reins, he heads off before I can thank him.

The church building is a picture-perfect sight bathed in soft sunlight. Its crisp white exterior gleams against the backdrop of a clear blue sky. The steeple rises tall while a weathered bell hangs gently within. I turn the knob on the door out of curiosity and I'm surprised to find it unlocked.

"Hello?"

Dust particles float through the air in the streams of sun

that flow in from the tall windows. The scent of pine and leather welcomes me. I set my bag down and move to the pulpit. Stretching out my arms, I grab onto the sides and look out over the pews imagining the faces staring back at me. *What am I doing here? I've gotten myself in way over my head.* I imagine stern judgmental faces peering back at me. They'll see right through me to the fraud that I am and know I have no right to be here.

"Oh, may I help you?" A woman's voice calls from behind me. I jump and grab my chest, almost stumbling over the stand.

"I do apologize," I say. "I'm Silas Flynn, the new preacher. I arrived only moments ago. I called out but no one answered, so I was just…" I'm fumbling over my words when I see the woman smile. "Here." I pull a letter from my pocket and hand it to her.

It's dirty and torn. She takes it as if reaching for a used handkerchief. I bite the inside of my lip as she slowly opens it. She inspects it with furrowed brows. I rub my hands together and shift my weight from one foot to the other.

"Reverend Flynn." She hands the missive back to me as if she's afraid to touch it. "I fear it's hard to read, but I trust it's the notification for you to join us as our newest pastor. I'm Roberta McCalister. It's so wonderful to finally meet you." She holds out her hand, which I'm happy to shake. "Do you have luggage?" she asks, looking around.

"Only a lone bag." I gesture to the back of the church where I left it.

"Let me show you to the parsonage."

"You caught me at a good time, Reverend. It just so happens that I came over to finish cleaning now that the Moores are gone. I was hoping to be finished before you arrived, and it appears you've come right on time." She seems to be a friendly enough woman, possibly the same age as my own mother, but she doesn't look as if life has dragged her down and through the mire as it had my ma. Missus McCalister produces a thin-lipped smile, which eases my nerves a touch. Although, I'm not sure how I feel about being called reverend.

"So, this is your new home," she exclaims, opening the door of the parsonage.

It's small but seems well cared for, and I am pleased with it. It's been a long time since I've had a place to call mine. I set my bag down and follow the woman as she shows me around. "I come over and clean every Friday morning at eight o'clock sharp." It doesn't take but a moment for her to lead us back to the kitchen where we began.

I consider telling her cleaning up after me isn't necessary, but she says it in a way that informs me there is no negotiating the subject.

"I won't be in your hair since I know you'll be at work at that time."

"Work?"

"Yes, surely the school informed you that the church board does not have the means to provide you with a salary large enough to live off?"

"Yes, of course. I'll start my search first thing tomorrow." Glancing about this humble home I sense sweat forming on my brow and I notice the top button of my shirt feels snugger than it had earlier. "How much is the rent?"

Her brows furrow. "Reverend, did they not teach you in seminary school that you live here at no charge?"

I chuckle with relief. "Of course, I'm afraid I can be a bit of a jokester, Missus McCalister, I do apologize."

Her lips curve into a grin.

I clear my throat. "I grew up working masonry. Do you know whom I may inquire about that?"

"Oh yes, that would be Bart Matthews. You'll find him working on the new bank building on Aspen Street."

"Thank you. I look forward to meeting him."

"Now, Brother Robert Simpson has agreed to take over church services until the end of the month to give you time to settle in and get acquainted with the church. Perhaps you should meet with him to apprentice until you take over the duties of the pastor."

"I shall do that," I respond, feeling more uneasy by the minute.

Before she leaves, she informs me that supper is at six o'clock "sharp" at her home. She points to the house visible beyond a line of trees from the kitchen window. She tells me their children are all grown and moved out, so most times it's only she and her husband. I want to tell her that having me is not necessary, but, much like the cleaning, I believe it's not an option. I'm feeling unsure that I like her as much now as I had when we met not twenty minutes ago.

When she's gone, I explore a little more thoroughly, opening drawers and cabinets. I find flour, beans, coffee, dishes...and a note pinned to the kitchen wall, "Rules for the Pastor." I sigh.

"Well, Silas, you asked for it," I whisper and turn from the pastoral *laws*.

11

Ginny

I strap Jake's revolver to my waist, hold his Spencer shotgun to my side, and call Buck to come. I've made target practice a part of my daily routine, and I'm proud of the fact that I've improved as a marksman. I'm nearly as good a shot as Old Man Marshall, and he almost never misses.

Buck and I are going over the ridge into Sutton's Creek today. I haven't left the camp in three years, since before Jake died. Normally I'd send the fellas with a list of supplies that I need, but this is something I must do on my own. With no plans on leaving the mountain, I must learn to fend for myself. If I die, well, I'll be with Jake that much sooner I reckon.

The sky is clear, not a cloud in sight, which is rare. One thing you can always count on is an afternoon rain shower this time of year. If I'm honest, what I fear more than bear or mountain lion is man. Man is the most dangerous beast of all.

There's an anxious feeling as I walk away from my property and the adjoining mining camp. Perhaps it's a mixture of fear and excitement. I've never taken this trip alone before. It's possible I won't return. Since it takes about half a day, and this is my first time, I've decided I'll get a room in town tonight. Thank goodness I have a little extra money for that. Jake and I always set out before sunrise and didn't return until after sunset. I'm not that brave on my own, fearing I may not see the trail and lose my way. The sun's done been up for about an hour now and the fellas have gone to work. I decided to wait so they didn't see and scold me for going without them. I made sure to leave a note on my door so they wouldn't worry. Well, they'll worry all right, but at least they'll know where to find me.

Although the laundress business brings in money, it's not a lot, and I believe I can do more. I've been working on hides and candles to trade and I'm hoping for a successful day of peddling. When I make it back to camp, I wish to at least be able to feel like the trip was worth it.

I have Jake's ma and sisters to thank for the hides and candles I have in my pack now. I don't believe I would've made the journey or built the life I have here, if it weren't for them.

"It'll be a grand adventure, Ginny." Jake's eyes were alight with excitement.

A rush of elation ran through me. "Yes. Oh, Jake." I wrapped my arms around him. "Yes, I'll marry you, and yes, I'll go anywhere you go."

Without my mother and father's blessing, we wed within days and lived with his family in their meager home while we gathered a wagon and supplies.

Living with the Price's was completely different from the life I had with my own parents, but I've never been happier than when Jake's family became mine. His ma taught me to cook and wash. His sisters taught me to sew and care for the animals. They taught me the art and skills I needed to live off the land. For the first time in my life, I learned how to milk cows and collect eggs. We had to cover the windows with quilts in the winter months to keep the cold wind out and the heat in. I'd never heard of such a thing before. But it was cozy, and there was true happiness in that home.

With the arrival of spring came our chance to leave with the wagon train.

Ma Price took Jake's face in her hands. "You take good care of our Ginny." Her cheeks were damp with tears.

Jake swiped under her eye with his thumb. "I will, Ma."

Carrie handed me a tin. "These biscuits and cookies should hold you over for several days." Her eyes were rimmed red and my heart squeezed when she handed the plate to me.

I pulled her in for a hug. "I'll write as often as I can." I drew back. "And you'll do the same?"

She sniffled and nodded.

In addition to the biscuits and cookies, his mother also sent us off with cake, while his sisters sent us off with quilts and curtains. My mother, on the other hand, sent a letter to Jake's parents about a week before we left, stating she heard what we were doing and how I'd regret it and come back. She ended it by writing, "mark my words."

Reaching the bustling mountain town, I'm brought back to the present and the realization I'm not exactly sure where to go. It's been a long time since I've set foot here, and I can see already how much has changed due to the growth. I head in the direction I believe the mercantile could be.

The door creaks and faces of men stare back at me. A few stand around in their finest suits and hats and a few with raggedy clothes and dirty countenances. They drink coffee and puff on pipes. The scent of tobacco fills the air and calms me. It's a familiar scent that I enjoy.

I must be a sight with my pack over my arm, one tucked under it, and a shotgun leaning on my shoulder. I imagine my hair has strayed, despite my straw hat and braid, and my face is flush. Buck dutifully trots behind me.

"Gentlemen." I smile, adjusting my eyes to the dim light of the room.

"Ma'am." They tip their hats and carry on with their conversation.

"How can I help you, young lady?" says the man behind the counter with the receding hairline and greased mustache. He looks a bit comical, and I bite back a chuckle. Perhaps that's the style in civilization now.

I place my packs on the counter. "I have hides and candles I'm hoping to trade."

"Well, let's see what you got there." He holds out his arms from across the counter to take my wares.

Once I'm loaded up with flour, sugar, beans, and some feminine items, I set out for the hotel. Mister Hanson, the store owner, said there were two hotels in town now, but one would be far cheaper for me if I'm willing to deal with a rowdier crowd. I grinned at his words and asked for directions. Little does he know that I live with a rowdy crowd every day at camp.

My packs are heavier now, and I'm thankful when I see the hotel sign. Tomorrow I'll have to figure out a way to redistribute my wares so they're not such a burden for the trek back home.

The hotel, if you can call it that, is positioned next door to a saloon. The paint of the building is chipped, and the sign is worn. When I enter, a strong pungent earthy scent assaults my nose. I can't place the smell, but I momentarily hold my breath. The bells hanging from the door ring out, and a little old woman with a brown complexion moves through a doorway filled with strands of colorful beads which make a tinkle sound as they clink against each other. A long messy braid hangs down her hunched back. and a pail lavender stone drapes over her neck.

There's a familiarity about her. As if I know her, but I don't. Perhaps I've seen her in town before.

Her face makes me think of when you crush a piece of paper into a ball and then try to smooth it out, not a single place without a wrinkle. She gives me the biggest toothless grin I've ever seen which makes my heart feel light and brings a wide smile to my own face.

"You're here for a room, sweetheart?"

"Do you have one available for the night?" I stare into her gray eyes wondering what kind of life she's lived.

She holds up two fingers. "I have *two* rooms available," she giggles.

"Well, I'm only in need of one."

She slowly takes a skeleton key from a hook on the wall behind the desk. "That'll be $1.50, sweetheart. Supper is down that hallway and to the right at six, and breakfast is in the same room tomorrow morning at seven. If you need water for washing up, let me know. I have a well out back. I can fetch you a pail and heat it for you. The outhouse is out that way as well. Knock before going in." She leans into the counter. "Some folks don't lock it. Can you imagine?" She laughs, giving the wood of the countertop a smack. "You'll be in room number four. Up those stairs and the second door on your right."

I'm unsure if she'll allow Buck to stay inside with me, but before I have an opportunity to ask, she states, "No worries about the dog, sweetheart. He'll be fine staying here with you." She cackles. "And I won't even charge you extra for him."

As I approach the steps, she calls out to me, "My name is Mirna. If you need anything, I'm happy to help if I'm able."

What a sweet lady.

The room is simple and clean with creaking floors. The strong earthy smell isn't as robust in this room, but I do feel in need of fresh air. When I attempt to open the window however, I find it's been painted shut. *Oh, fiddlesticks!*

A man's voice and the giggles of a woman from the room next door are as if we're practically in the same space. I stare out the window watching the people below, wondering who they are and where they're going, when suddenly the sounds of slight banging and moaning come from my neighbors. I smile to myself at the thought of someone having pleasure in the middle of the day. I must admit I feel a bit like a Peeping Tom which gives me an uncomfortable sensation, but also a bit of jealousy I suppose.

I do wish to wash up, but I can't imagine or expect that old woman to carry a heavy pail of water for me. This would be a good time to go downstairs and see if I can fetch it myself.

I sit at a tiny table in Mirna's equally tiny living space while my bucket of bath water heats on her cookstove.

"What brings you to Sutton's Creek?" she asks, filling my cup with steaming hot tea.

"I live near a camp about half a day's journey over the ridge. This is my first time coming to town by myself since…" I cradle the cup in my hands watching the liquid swirl.

"Since your husband died." She pats my shoulder and pours tea into her cup.

"Yes." There's a pitch in my tone. How would she know that? Do I look like a widow?

She points behind me. "He's with you."

"Pardon?" The hairs on my arm stand and I turn expecting to see Jake there.

Her toothless smile hasn't wavered once. "He's with you, sweetheart. I can see him."

I'm unsure if I should run or ask questions. Intrigue fastens me to my seat, although goosebumps have formed on my arms.

My face must show surprise because she giggles. "I'm *gifted*, as my mother would say."

"I don't understand. Are you a witch?" She does look as I've always imagined a witch to appear, partially. Scraggly gray hair, wrinkled face, and now she's telling me she can see my dead husband.

She laughs and pushes a plate of cookies towards me. "The *gift*, it runs in my family, my mother's side." She runs her hand over a section of the tablecloth as if smoothing it out even though it doesn't need to be. "It's not something I let be known to many." Her gray eyes twinkle. "Most people don't understand such things. They fear it, and they destroy what they fear. But your husband, his name starts with a J."

I nod. "Jake." The goosebumps reappear.

"He's telling me you'll be understanding of my gift. You've questioned it yourself, if you have a gift of knowing. Yes, sweetheart, if you wish for it to, in time it shall grow stronger. But you must practice."

I think of how I originally sensed that Jake sent Buck to me.

"My dog?" The animal who lays at my feet snores gently.

She bobs her head. "Jake says you were going to die if he didn't do something to bring you back to life. Yes, he brought your dog to you."

Instantly I think of what Joe and I had done, and fear grips me. Had he seen us? Had he seen Joe and me in our…my and Jake's bed?

"You have nothing to be ashamed of, he's reassuring you. You've done nothing wrong. He wishes for you to know you deserve to be loved and cared for." She leans forward and places a cold crinkled hand over mine. "A love shall come, and when he does, you have Jake's blessing."

I stare at the stone that hangs from her neck by a leather cord. This moment feels so unreal, as if I'm outside my body watching this conversation happen. This isn't the first time I've experienced this feeling.

"So, he's in heaven?" Afterlife has baffled me since Jake died. Before it was black and white. Heaven and hell. But I've questioned that since he left.

"I suppose you could call it heaven if you like."

"Is there a hell?"

"No. There is only the other side. No up or down, in or out, only the other side. Imagine there's a curtain between you and me. You wouldn't be able to see me fully, but you'd know I was there, wouldn't you?"

I nod.

"You feel your husband."

I nod again.

"Yes, that's because he's there. You've questioned it, but you already know his soul is still very much alive, only not in his earthly body. Our bodies are but houses that our spirits dwell in. Some day we must move out, but we're still living."

"Will he always be with me? Shall he stay with me, from the other side?"

"He'll be there whenever you need him to be there. He says you visit his grave, and that's all right, but you don't have to. When you think of him or speak to him, he's there, wherever you are."

This strange little old lady has settled my heart. I'm so thankful I made the trek into town, that this was the hotel I was directed to, and that she had a room available for me. It's at this moment I know Jake guided me here.

The next morning, with a full belly and a rested body and

spirit, I thank Mirna for her hospitality. Above all, I'm thankful for her confirming everything I knew but questioned. Her confirmations about Jake, heaven, the Bible, and God.

"May I hug you?" I ask from across the counter, my packs and Buck sitting on the floor at my feet.

"If you hadn't asked me, I'd have asked you." She shuffles her way around the wooden barrier and brings me into the strongest hug she can muster. "Oh, I almost forgot," she declares.

I watch her shuffle back through her beaded doorway and grab a small package wrapped in brown paper tied with string.

"Mountain sage," she says. "Burn this on a plate or slab of wood in your house and say a blessing, sending any bad energy out the open door." She waves one hand over the other demonstrating the sweeping of something away. Then she removes the stone from around her neck. "This is for you."

"Oh, I can't take this."

"I insist." She raises the necklace up to place it over my head, so I bend forward to receive it. "This stone shall awaken your soul to your highest powers, sweetheart, the powers you call God, and shall protect you from negative energies."

I hold it in my fingers, light glinting off its jagged edges. "I don't know what to say."

She takes my hand in hers. "Your husband has given you a gift. Treasure it."

Unsure whether she's referring to the necklace, Buck, or the gift of communicating with Jake, I settle on treasuring them all.

As I trudge my way back to home, I can't help but think about Mirna saying I'd find love again and that I have Jake's blessing. I wonder if this means Joe is returning. New men in search of a more favorable life do come through occasionally. Perhaps he, whoever he is, is on his way.

12

Silas

Sweat dampens my pillow as I toss and turn. It's never easy for me to sleep in a new place. Of course, I often find myself sleeping with one eye open. The moonlight streams in and the shadows of the trees dance off the walls, an eerie feeling. It's ironic that I'm living in a church parsonage, yet I don't feel safe. Evil's presence lurks. It's always around, like air, it never leaves. It's been this way for me since I was a child. I find myself grappling with the echoes of my past, which seem to haunt me. A punishment from God.

I used to pray until I fell asleep, but praying doesn't seem to do the trick for me anymore. I'm so lonely and it feels as if God is a million miles away, if He exists at all.

I wonder if they allow dogs here at the parsonage. I didn't see anything about no dogs on the *Rules for the Pastor*, but I'll ask Mister and Missus McCalister. Perhaps a companion of the four-legged kind is what I need.

I find my way to Aspen Street and ask for Bart Matthews. A stout man chewing on a cigar shakes my hand.

"I know you're the new preacher and all, but I'd be obliged if you keep that at church and let my men be themselves." His cigar still clenched between his teeth.

If only he knew me. "Yes sir, I can respect that."

"Good. Can you start now?" He looks me over.

The sounds of hammering and the scraping of mortar fill the air around the worksite.

"I brought my lunch pail in hopes you'd say that."

"Well, let's get you to work. If you do a good job today, I'll hire you. Fair?"

"Yes, sir."

He scrunches his nose. "And stop calling me sir."

I laugh. "As long as you call me Silas and not preacher or reverend."

The man grins and extends his hand. "I believe we have a deal, Silas."

A younger man beside me whistles as I roll my sleeves. "I've never seen a preacher with arms like those." He shakes his head. "Reverend Moore was an old fat man."

"Blast it, Calvin, don't be talking about a reverend like that, especially to the new preacher."

I already miss being treated like everyone else. Being a part of this group of men is something I wish for. I detest the hushed voices because "the preachers here." I feel like an outcast, and I'm unsure if I'll ever get used to it. I understand it, though, and I must live with it as it's the lot I've chosen.

Laughing, I say, "It's all right. I'm a man just like you. Masonry, mostly, is how I got these arms. I grew up farming, but my father was a mason, and he had me out working since the day I was able to lift a stone."

"I'm George," says the man who rebuked Calvin. He holds out his hand to me.

"Please, call me Silas."

The first day working for Bart Matthews erecting the new bank building for future business was a success. The way I worked with my hands earned me the respect of the men. I must admit, I found myself feeling like a leper once again when the day was done, and they agreed to meet at the saloon for a drink.

I came home, cleaned up, and had a mostly silent supper with the McCalisters. I'll see how living here goes, but I'm not planning to remain in this town for more than a month or two, long enough to save up extra money.

As it turned out, the church board preferred no dogs live at the parsonage, but they were fine with cats. I've never been much for cats, but they do keep the mice at bay, so I asked Calvin where I could get one. He was more than happy to bring me a female feline this evening. She's gray and seems to have a good disposition. As I read the Bible by lamplight, she curls up in my lap. I pet her and give thanks I'm no longer alone. "I think I'll call you Naomi, after my mama. Would that be all right? Naomi," I say the name, trying it out. Yes, it fits. She's gentle and loving, just like my ma.

As I think of my mother, I wonder how she is, if she's in good health and happy. It's been a long time since I've stayed in one place long enough to receive a letter from her. I know she frets over me. All she ever dreamt was the best for me. As long as I can allow her to believe that, I shall.

The cat purrs gently as I brush my hand over her soft fur. "I think I'll keep you."

She licks her paw, oblivious to what befalls us humans in this world.

13

Silas

The heat of the day bakes me as though I were in an oven. My muscles are sore and tired from mixing mortar and laying bricks all morning. Standing, I stretch my fatigued arms.

Bart slaps my back. "I'd say it's time for a dinner break."

"Sounds good to me."

We head to the well that sits some yards away from our work site, drawing water to wash our hands and wet our parched tongues. Then we sit in a grove of aspens that line the back lot.

As he does every day during the midday meal break, George pulls out a deck of cards and begins dealing them out.

I fan mine in front of my face to get a good look as I bite into my buttered pork sandwich that I made for myself this morning.

When I first began working with these men several weeks ago, I hated to see my presence taking away their enjoyment. I made it known that I was here to work, not judge. Whatever preconceived notions they had about me, they could forget. They now appear to enjoy having me around. They would take the shirts off their own backs for me, I'm sure of it.

A wagon pulls up from behind us and I see that it's Connor Murphy, the banker, and his daughter, Bridget. The men and I share glances.

"Gentlemen," Mister Murphy calls from atop his seat. "How's the progress?"

Bart shakes Mister Murphy's hand then tips his hat to Bridget. "Ma'am."

"It's coming right along. Thankfully the weather's been cooperating."

"Good to hear." Mister Murphy peers over at the rest of us. "Keep up the good work men." He nods to Bart and guides his team back down the road.

As I do most every night, I find myself eating a silent dinner at the McCalisters. Only the clinking of dishes can be heard, besides the thoughts that whir in my head. This evening's meal consists of pork roast, green beans, fried potatoes, and sliced bread.

"I hear the new building for the bank is right on track to be completed on time." Mister McCalister surprises me with the statement, being a man of very few words.

"Yes sir. Connor Murphy came by today and Mister Matthews reassured him it's coming along."

Mister McCalister clears his throat. "Reverend Flynn." He

sits his fork on his plate. "I heard some disturbing news today."

I'm puzzled about what this news could be. "Sir?"

"I hear you were playing cards this afternoon."

Here we go. "Yes, sir."

Missus McCalister leans her fork on her plate and sits back in her chair, hands in her lap and head down. *Quite an odd thing to do.*

Mister McCalister shakes his head.

I recall the "Rules for the Pastor" stating there was to be no gambling. "We weren't wagering for money, only playing a simple card game. The winner gets nothing but bragging rights."

"Cards lead to gambling."

I sit back in my chair and run my palms down the thighs of my slacks. This has Bridget Murphy's fingerprints all over it. I've never done anything to that girl. She seems to enjoy causing trouble all over town.

Mister McCalister holds up his hand. "Now, I realize you're still a young preacher and have a lot to learn. Although I can't promise no one else won't, I've decided I won't tell the rest of the men on the board. Just consider this a warning, a lesson to be learned."

I nod. Though my appetite is completely gone, I respectfully finish my supper, but also respectfully decline dessert and head back to the parsonage.

Just like when I was a child, I can't seem to do anything right.

My thoughts, unbidden, return to a day when my mother sent me out back to gather berries for her church picnic pie—a task that has carried with it a weight I can't seem to shake.

I place a few berries in my bucket, and I eat a few. Before I know it, my bucket and my belly are full, so I make my way back through the berry patch, over the field, and to our little cabin. When I open the door, my father grabs me by the arm and begins wailing on me with his strap. The bucket slips from my hands, sending berries scattering across the floor. In our dance of him lashing me while I twist and turn to avoid the blows, most of the berries are trampled right into my mother's floor.

It was only after he'd given me a good whipping that I learned he'd been calling for me, and when I failed to answer, he took it to mean I was deliberately ignoring him.

I can't help but wonder if I'll ever find peace in my life.

As I reflect on the injustices of my childhood, anger wells within me. Yet, there is also a sense of gratitude, knowing that the man who hurt me can no longer do so. But now, it feels as though the church board is no better than my father.

14

Ginny

This is my last planned trip over the ridge before winter comes. Visiting Mirna once every four or five weeks has become customary. We have tea while she educates me on herbal remedies. We discuss Jake and how he and I communicate with each other. I don't see him as she does, but I feel him. And although I can't hear him as I hear the crunch of gravel and sticks under my boots now as I walk the trail, I do hear him clearly. Thinking about it brings a smile to my face.

It's a splendid morning as Buck and I set out on the trail. Jake's guns, one on my belt and one slung over my shoulder, are my source of protection. And Buck shall alert me if anything's amiss, which I'm grateful for.

The fellas aren't keen on me going into town alone, but they respect my wishes to let me do this on my own. We've agreed that if I don't return within three days' time then they'll come looking for me.

It's quiet as we stroll along the stony dirt path. I have never seen a country with so many rocks. *Nothing's smooth here, and I truly could use a new pair of boots* I think as my ankle twists on the trail debris. Buck waits for me to catch up. *Thank you, Jake, for sending Buck to me.* It's a phrase I repeat often.

My visits to Jake's gravesite are daily. Every morning, I go to his body's resting place, the mound high with rocks, and speak with him. I know he's not there, but it's a ritual I've grown accustomed to. He's right proud of me and Buck, and he's happy that I didn't go back to New York to my parents. That's what Mirna's confirmed for me. *"It would have been a terrible decision."*

That one simple remark stirs up a memory from my childhood.

Mother screams at Ella, one of our servants, ordering her to do something. Miss Ella pounds Father's back while I attempt feverishly to scoop steak from his throat. Ella and I sob as Father turns a deep shade of blue before he finally coughs up the meat which shoots out across his plate. Mother sits with both hands on the table, just staring in shock. Not a tear in her eye. In fact, I'd never once seen her shed a tear for anyone. All she seemed to care about was money, property, and what would happen to her if Father died. I couldn't help but wonder if she was sorry he didn't.

After some time, I stop to rest on a tree stump while Buck drinks from the canteen. I'm careful to pour it above him so he doesn't lick the opening. Having water in these mountains is a must. I get thirstier and my skin gets drier and itchier than it did back in New York. The mountain air is different, I suppose. Or maybe it's because we're up so high. I guess the reason doesn't much matter.

My feet are hurting something awful by the time we reach the mercantile. Sitting on the bench outside, I lay my hat on my lap and recline my head against the building. "I just need a moment, Buck."

He lounges at my feet content to take a little siesta himself. I close my eyes, feeling the warmth of the sun kissing my face since this building doesn't have a covered porch.

When I hear a woman inquiring about a job and a place to stay, my ears perk up the way Buck's do when I mention food or going outside. An idea forms. It may be crazy. She may say no. But I must give it a try. Perhaps this is a nudge from Jake. Mirna always says to listen to my heart.

"Excuse me, miss," I call to the woman as she walks away, looking defeated. She's young, my age I'm guessing, and her reddish blonde hair is pulled back into a chignon.

"Yes?" She turns to me, and I hesitate, almost losing my nerve.

"I'm hiring." I'm not. I can hardly get by myself, but this might be a winning situation for the both of us. "It's not much," I continue. "I'll pay you in room and board. I live just over the ridge there on the outskirts of the mining camp. It's small and not fancy in the least, but it's cozy enough. And I'll give you a tenth of what the men pay me."

"What is it you do?" the woman asks.

"I'm a laundress." A laundress? *Well aren't you fancy now, Virginia?* "It's not glamorous by any means." She can conceive that by the looks of me. A tattered skirt, broken down boots, and chapped hands clutching a dirty straw hat. "I wash the miners' clothing. And they're right good men. Gentlemen. Like family." I'm stammering, attempting my best to convince her it's safe to come home with me.

The woman holds out her hand. "Olivia Palmer. Please call me Livvie."

I smile. "Ginny Price. And this here's Buck." He's sniffing around Livvie's skirts which makes her laugh.

"Are you married?" she asks.

"I'm widowed," I say, matter-of-fact.

Her smile grows wider. "So am I," she says sweetly. "I suppose it's a deal then." With her hand still extended out to me, we shake on it.

"I have to get some supplies from the mercantile and visit a friend, then we can be on our way." I look down toward her feet although her skirts cover them. "You got good boots on?"

"As good as they're going to get." She lifts her skirts and points the toe of her shoe at me. "I'll manage. I've lived with worse. Come on, I'll help you carry what you need." She walks past me toward the door of the store.

Something tells me this is my lucky day. Who knew I'd find a new friend when I came to town? I place my hand over my heart and murmur a quiet thank you.

15

Silas

I've been invited to the Petersons' for the Thanksgiving meal—a family I treasure, and yet, I can't shake the feeling that I'm not exactly excited to go. The weight of a hidden burden is heavy on me. Not because of my morals, or lack thereof, but because I've grown to genuinely love this family and their nephew Justus Bennett. Justus and I are so similar. I wish I could tell him, but that would mean revealing so much of who I am. My past must remain where it's at, behind me.

Sitting in the rocker, I peer out on the fresh snow that's fallen overnight. The thought of starting over makes me wince, but I believe it's time. I've been here much longer than anticipated. I believed I was ready to settle down, but the pull to leave and explore nags at me. Perhaps there's room for me further west, California maybe.

Stroking Naomi's fur, I take a sip from my steaming mug

and the bitterness bites my tongue. I've never learned to make a decent cup of coffee.

As the cat sleeps contentedly in my lap, I debate whether I should take her with me or if I should give her back to Calvin. I'll miss her something awful if I leave her behind, but I'm unsure if taking her with me would be the best thing for her.

The thud of a log falling inside the woodstove brings me back to my current situation, getting dressed to have supper with the Petersons. Once I collect my pay on Friday, I'll leave this town behind, just as I've done countless times before. Restlessness seems to be in my nature.

I'm greeted at Doc and Miss Bea's door by their son-in-law, Clint.

"Silas. I'm glad you came." He pats my shoulder and motions for me to place my coat and scarf on the rack beside the door. "Let's get you a cup of coffee to warm up." He limps down the hall towards the kitchen.

Clint was injured when he and Justus joined the war together as teens. Justus has suffered a tremendous amount of guilt about it over the years.

Miss Bea buzzes around the kitchen while Clint's very pregnant wife, Hannah, sets the table and Rebecca, removing rolls from the oven, gives me a smile. "Silas, we're so happy you could come."

"Thank you all for inviting me. It smells wonderful in here."

Rebecca, I've come to learn, is an ex-slave taken in by Doc

and Miss Bea on their travels out here to the Colorado Territory. Rebecca had been sold separately from her husband and twin daughters. She has no idea where they are, nor do they know Rebecca was pregnant with her now eight-year-old son Thomas at the time.

Miss Bea throws her hands in the air. "Oh, Silas. Clint's getting you coffee, good. We're almost ready to eat. Justus is in the front room, go on and join him."

Justus, with an ankle propped on one knee, is reading a newspaper. His boots are worn as you'd expect a rancher's shoes to be and there's an indentation in his dirty blonde hair from where his hat normally rests.

"Happy Thanksgiving, Justus."

He jumps up sitting the paper down in his seat. "Silas, Happy Thanksgiving." He holds out his hand to shake mine. "Although I'm still unsure what there is to be thankful for. Stealing Indian land?"

I nod. "Perhaps the focus could be on an abundant harvest and good health."

"I suppose you're right."

Having a seat beside Justus on the sofa, I can't help thinking about how much he must be hurting today despite his smile.

He fell in love with a woman, Olivia Palmer, who was living here with his aunt and uncle, Doc and Miss Bea. Olivia had quite the abusive past that she couldn't seem to free herself from, and despite Justus's love and reassurances to her, she recently chose to leave Laurel Springs.

There was a girl once, and I was certain I would marry her — before the incident occurred and forced Ma and me to leave town. I can still see the pain on Clementine's face when I told her I was leaving. She couldn't understand, and even I struggled to fully grasp it myself.

We meet in our usual spot, a clearing in the woods on my parents' property. When she sees me, Clem's eyes are alight. Her blonde hair, half up and half down, trail her arms in loose ringlets. She runs to me with her skirts hiked. My heart feels as though someone were squeezing the life out of it. This is it. This is the price I must pay for what I've done.

She must see the agony on my face because her smile falls. "What is it, Silas?"

Leaves murmur in the breeze.

"I'm sorry, Clem, but Mama's making me live with my brother, Jody."

"Well, I'll miss you of course, but you'll come back, and we'll marry then." She searches my eyes.

I hang my head and run the lace of her blouse between my finger and thumb. "She's going too. We're not returning."

"You can return." Her tone is hopeful.

"I can't, Clem. I'm sorry." She doesn't know what I've done, and I can't tell her. This is between me, Ma, and God.

Tears roll down her face, and I let her weep against my chest.

"I'm so sorry." I smooth my hand over her head and down her back allowing her to cry.

With watery eyes, she peers up at me and her mouth lifts at the corners in a soft smile. "One last time, please." I taste her salty tears when she places her lips on mine. Our bodies, bare and tangled on the ground, share a closeness that is both heart-wrenching and beautiful, a connection that feels more profound than ever before.

Despite searching for that feeling again, I have yet to find it.

Now, eight years later as I think of that day, I wonder what ever happened to Clementine. There's no doubt she married another, most likely she's a mother now too.

"You're quieter than usual," says Justus, bringing me out of my memories. "And that's saying a lot since you're pretty quiet as it is."

I contemplate telling him what's on my mind, leaving Laurel Springs.

"What is it, my friend?" Justus shifts his body and places one arm on the back of the sofa.

I should be consoling him over Olivia leaving just when he was about to propose, but instead he's ready to hear my woes. Justus has been a better friend to me than anyone ever has my whole life, even my ole Irish buddy Stephen. There's nothing Justus wants or needs from me but companionship. I've come to learn the man that he is, and I know he'd give the coat off his own back in a blizzard if he thought it'd save someone else's life.

I decide this is a confession I can't make now. Justus is still human, and I'll always know that he knows.

"I suppose I'm feeling a bit alone here, that's all." It's not what I wish to say but it's not an untruth either.

"So, you're ready to find a wife? Have you met any prospects in the church?"

I think of all the married or elderly women who sit before me during my sermons. There are some young ladies whose fathers would happily marry them to the new preacher, but no, I need a woman. I think of Bridget Murphy with her high and mighty airs. When I first met her, I thought she was beautiful but quickly saw through her outward beauty to her judgmental mind and greedy heart.

I laugh. "No." I say point blank.

"It's a small town and an even smaller congregation you have, *Reverend*." Justus emphasizes the last word with a smile. "I know you just arrived, but have you thought about moving to a bigger town? Denver maybe?" He moves his arm from the back of the sofa to his lap causing the newspaper to make a crumpling sound. "Not that I want you to leave," he adds quickly. "For selfish reasons, I hope you stay. But life's too short to be unhappy."

I cock my head and my mouth thinking about the same question I run through my mind day after day. *What do I want? What should I do?* "I don't know, Justus. I love Laurel Springs." This has become the safest unsafe option for me.

"Well, there's no doubt you'll figure it out. Also, might I add you take your own advice and make room for that future bride?" Justus raises his coffee mug to me before taking a drink.

I recall that one sermon Justus attended when I had the old ladies in church so upset that I dared to tell them to take God at his word. I told them if they wished for a child to sew a blanket for that little one even though they weren't here yet. I told them if they were sick to speak healing over their bodies. And if they wished for love, to make room in their home for that man or woman.

Justus is right, I need to take my own advice and go home and make room for my future wife. But then the question becomes, do I care to marry someone in the church? Do I wish to marry someone who would be a dutiful preacher's wife? I don't know how much longer I can keep up this illusion I'm living.

I also haven't been with a woman in a long while, and it's not easy when I remember the wonderful touch of one. My need began with the ladies at Mister Wells's saloon, where the warmth of their presence lingered longer than I care to admit.

Mister Wells hired me as a boy to help care for his establishment doing things such as sweep, scrub floors, wash glasses, clean windows, and take care of spittoons. Some of the ladies there weren't much older than I was at the time, and they didn't mind teaching me a thing or two in their private bedrooms. In the beginning, they did it without taking money from me, but when Mister Wells found out he said if I were going to use his girls then he'd take it out of my pay.

I can still smell the rosewater at the thought of Pearl. Her skin was like porcelain and her touch just as delicate. Oh, how she loved pleasuring me while I watched. She preferred it because it meant she didn't have to bathe afterward. She could glide back down the stairs and take any man who wanted her.

Mister Wells wasn't keen on my time with the Hubbard sisters and would take triple from my pay because they were his biggest money makers. The Hubbard sisters were identical twins who always took a man together. The things those girls did and taught me would make a grown man blush.

Then there was Miss Ophelia. She was like a mother to the women and oversaw everything they did. She was plump with gigantic breasts and oh, boy was she a fine teacher in the art of fornication.

The night before my father succumbed to his death, I was working at the saloon.

I hadn't seen my father come in that night. Usually, he played cards and drank until I had to help him home because he was so drunk. But on this night, I come in from dumping a spittoon and see him at the top of the stairs. Miss Ophelia runs her fingers over her overflowing bosoms, peering up at my father like a schoolgirl. He slides money into the top of her plunging dress, whispers something in her ear that makes her giggle, and then he heads down the stairs. I burn with fury. Not that he is bedding a woman I've been with, but that he is doing this while my ma is most certainly fretting and praying that he makes it home tonight.

I glance away before he can notice me noticing him. Grabbing another spittoon, I slip back outside.

Remembering my manners, I turn my attention back to Justus. "Any word from Olivia?"

He lowers his pained eyes. "I've written to her, but she won't respond. Sometimes I tell myself she's not getting my letters, but she's staying in contact with my aunt and Rebecca, so I know she's only disregarding me."

"She's deeply wounded."

"I didn't even do anything I shouldn't have," he says in frustration. "She thought she saw something she didn't and left me." He folds the paper up and swats his knee with it.

"It has to be more than that. She's got a lot to work through. Maybe in time?"

"She doesn't trust men. Men have hurt her all her life. Why would I be any different?"

I think of how I betrayed Clementine by having relations with the women at the saloon and wonder if I'm any better than my father.

I shake my head. "I'm sorry, Justus."

He plays with a corner of the newspaper. "Such is life, I suppose. I reckon she's better off without me."

"I wouldn't say that."

Justus shrugs. "There's nothing else I can do, Silas, to help her see I'm not like all the other no-good men in her life, starting with her stepfather."

"I know she loves you. Perhaps she only needs time—."

My words are cut short when young Thomas comes running into the room with Clint and Hannah's two little ones, Chet and Mimi, on his heels.

"Mama says it's time to eat," says Thomas.

"Yeth, it's tine to eat," Mimi repeats in her tiny voice.

Justus takes the little girl into his arms. "I guess we better listen to Miss Rebecca, hadn't we?"

When supper's over, I head out into the cold evening air with two plates of leftovers. As I trudge down the porch Justus steps out behind me.

"Silas."

I turn just as he claps his hand on my shoulder. "Thanks for being a good friend. I know you're not only my friend in an attempt to get me to attend church or *give my life to the Lord.* I know you're a genuine friend and I appreciate it. It's strange. I won't lie about that." He laughs and pats my back. "I don't know what I'd do without you."

"Thank you, Justus. That means a lot to me. Being the preacher tends to keep friends away."

"Well, you can't keep me away." He untethers his horse

from the hitching post. "Have a good night."

"Good night to you."

As I walk back to the parsonage, I contemplate if I should reconsider leaving town and instead make Laurel Springs my home after all.

16

Ginny

"Jake, thank you so much for sending Livvie to me," I say with excitement as I place my arms over the mound of stones where his body is buried. "She's turned out to be like the sister I never had." I clutch the lavender stone that still hangs about my neck. It's usually tucked inside my blouse, so I won't lose it, but sometimes I have a need to feel it's energy in my hand.

I can hear Jake laugh. *She needs you right now as much as you need her.* Then I sense he's confirming what I believe to have known for a few weeks now. Livvie's with child.

"Why hasn't she told me?" I wonder aloud.

She's afraid to tell you.

"Oh, Jake, we're going to have a baby," I squeal. "There's so much to be done: sewing clothing, knitting blankets…" I chew my lip. "I bet one of the fellas would make a cradle," I exclaim in excitement.

Jake's laughter caresses my ears once again. I've always been able to make him laugh, and it makes my heart smile.

Once back to the cabin, Livvie and I set to preparing breakfast before starting on the wash. As much as I care for her, I can't understand why she won't go back to Justus. It's obvious he loves her from the stories she's told me, not to mention the letters he writes. Oh, how I'd give anything to have Jake here with me, to see his face and have him hold me in his arms. I miss his smile something terrible at times.

Livvie places her hand to her stomach. "I'm sorry, Ginny, but I need to go outside. The smell of the bacon is making me feel wretched. I must be coming down with something." She steps out the door and I nod my head in realization that this is another sign of what I've known. This is the same thing that happened to me when I was pregnant. I felt terribly ill, and the smell of animal fat made it even worse.

I toast a slice of bread in the oven and take it outside to my friend, who leans against a tree facing out over the magnificent mountain range. When the sun brushes over it in the early morning, the landscape has a purple hue that is so lovely. This beautiful view is exactly why Jake chose this very spot to build our home.

"This should help." I hand Livvie the bread.

She gives me half a smile. "Thank you."

"You were intimate with Justus, weren't you?" She pulls a bite sized piece from the toast. "I know it's a bold question to ask, but given how close we've become, I want you to know there's no judgment." I lean against the tree beside her. "Jake and

I sure couldn't wait until our wedding night. I don't believe in all that anyway. What if he's no good? Then you marry someone who shall never please you. That's no way to live." I nudge her shoulder with mine.

Livvie giggles.

I pick at the bark on the tree, thinking of Joe. "I was almost with someone else after Jake died. His name is Joe. And he'll always be someone I hold dear. He wanted to marry me, but it wouldn't have been fair to either of us, so he chose to leave camp."

Livvie's still peering out over the rolling hills of evergreens, aspens, and boulders. "I've never known any man like Justus. Oh, Ginny, I've ruined everything."

I wrap my arm around her and rest a hand on her belly. "You carry a part of him with you."

"Yes, he shall forever hold a cherished place in my heart."

"No. Livvie, look at me." I turn her to face me and gaze into her blue eyes. Again, I rest a hand on her stomach. "I know you're carrying Justus's child."

She sighs and slumps against the tree. "How did you know?"

"I've been where you are. I know the signs. And I believe we need to take you into town and call on the midwife." I grin. "*We're* going to have a baby."

Tears well in her eyes and her hand covers her mouth. There's a smile behind that hand and I lean in and hug my dear sweet friend.

When we reach the midwife in Sutton's Creek, the woman confirms what we already knew. Livvie's pregnant.

Mirna offers both ginger and peppermint to be used as a tea

to help with the nausea but then reassures us it should pass in a few weeks.

"I don't understand how this is possible. I was with Roy for years and never got pregnant." Livvie says to the old woman, regarding her deceased husband.

"Sometimes it's the man that can't get the woman pregnant, sweetheart." Mirna pats the back of Livvie's hand. "You got yourself a man with powder in his gun now." She gently squeezes Livvie's cheek and smiles her toothless grin.

I can't help but burst into laughter and Livvie looks at me with wide amused eyes. "I'm sorry," I say, glancing at Mirna who gives me a wink.

Watching Livvie, I can't help but wonder if this will send her back to Laurel Springs, leaving me alone once again.

17

Ginny

Moisture covers the window of the cabin, a sign of the freezing snow blowing outside and the warmth of the fire inside. The aroma of venison stew simmering from the pot on the stove fills the little room.

Although it's Sunday, there's never a respite from work around here. There's always wash to be done, patches to be sewn, or food to be prepared. Today, however, is one of those days that feels like being wrapped in a warm blanket, and I find myself missing jovial celebrations from my childhood. The holidays are soon approaching, and I imagine Mother's servants hanging wreaths on each window and door.

I recall the Christmas Jake and I spent living with his family before traveling west. His sisters and I made gingerbread and fried cakes. The simple tree Jake and his father brought from the woods, we ladies adorned with ribbon and strands of popped corn. It was the best Christmas I'd experienced in my life, because there was love.

Closing the oven, I glance about. Livvie is reclined on the bed stitching a tear in a shirt, and Buck, per usual, naps near the stove. There's never been room in this cabin for a tree, but I'm yearning for one.

The faint sounds of voices carry from outside, and I figure it's the fellas doing any number of things, fetching water from the creek, going to or returning from town, hunting, or collecting firewood.

"I was thinking, for Christmas this year we could decorate a sapling. There's plenty to choose from."

Livvie lays her sewing in her lap.

"Even a seedling wouldn't fit in here."

I pull a chair from the table and have a seat. "We could decorate it out there. We can make ornaments from tallow and seeds, which would be both festive and provide food for the birds."

"That's a splendid idea."

Livvie sets the shirt aside and caresses her belly. "I dare say I could take a nap right now."

Jumping up, I crack open the oven door to peek in on the bread. "Johnny cakes are almost done. You should eat first."

Livvie moans. "The stew does smell wonderful. I'm thankful to Old Man Marshall for bringing the deer meat down."

A pounding at the door startles us.

Assuming it's one of the fellas, I open it but find two men covered in firs and snow.

"Sorry to arrive unannounced, ma'am, but we've been

walking for hours in this storm. Would you mind if we come in and warm up a bit? We'll be on our way in no time." The burly man takes up much of the entrance.

I'm about to send them to the camp when a petite woman steps out from behind him, her eyes sunken and her cheeks red.

"Of course. Please come in. Have a seat at the table." I gesture for them to sit. "You all look as though you could use a bowl of stew."

Livvie moves from the bed. "I'll start coffee."

"Folks call me Sully," says the burly man taking a seat. "This is my brother, Jim, and our sister, Fern."

"She don't talk much," says Jim.

The woman brushes a frail hand over the part in her hair, keeping her eyes downcast.

"It's nice to meet you folks. I'm Ginny, and this is Livvie." I spoon the meaty stew into a bowl. "Where you all heading?"

"Sutton's Creek," replies Sully.

When lowering the bowl to place it in front of Fern, Sully snatches it from my hands and begins eating like a wolf to a carcass.

"That's a good four-hour journey on a clear day."

Jim snickers. "Perhaps you could let us stay until the morning."

I glance to Livvie.

"We can sleep on the floor. The storm'll be lifted by then." Jim holds out his hand to retrieve the cup of coffee from Livvie, but she passes him and sits it before Fern.

"I'm afraid we don't have the room." I point in the direction of the camp. "But I'm certain the miners just up the hill will have a place for you for the night."

Fern shrugs out of her coat. Her belly is large and round with child. Both Sully and Jim eye her with anger and she slinks into the chair.

"Perhaps your sister can stay the night with us," I say. "The camp isn't much of a place for a woman."

"She stays with us," Sully replies, licking Johnny cake crumbs from his thumb.

Jim trails a finger along the sparse chinking between the logs. "It appears you two could use menfolk around here."

"We manage just fine." Livvie's voice is laced with confidence, but she peers at me with concern.

I recall the incident with the two men, Bill and Clarance, and how Marsh shot them dead for attempting to rape me. With my bowl of stew, I sit on my bed near my shotgun that's propped against the wall. What happened then won't happen now.

Jim rests his arm on the table. "It would do Fern here good to be around womenfolk."

"There's plenty of women in Sutton's Creek. Perhaps she'll find a companion there," I counter.

A whimper sends my attention to Fern. Sully has her by the back of the neck. "You finish every last bite, you hear?"

Jim's relaxed in his seat, tapping on the table.

I set my bowl on the floor and grab my rifle. In two quick steps I have it cocked and held against the back of Sully's head. He raises both his hands.

"I believe you best be on your way."

He chuckles. "I didn't mean no harm, just keeping the little lady in line that's all. She tends to be impolite."

I kick the leg of the chair. "I said, I believe you best be on your way." I move the gun between the two men while giving them room to remove themselves from my table and my home.

The wind blows against the house and the tinkle from the icy snow brushes the glass.

"You're making a big mistake here," Sully chides.

I press the butt of the gun harder into my shoulder. "No, you are if you don't leave, now."

"Come on, woman," Sully sneers at Fern, who remains cowering in the chair.

"She stays."

Fern's gaze lifts at Livvie's words.

Jim cackles, "Naw, she comes with us." He pulls at the woman's arm, and she peers up at Livvie while shrugging into her coat.

"She stays," Livvie repeats.

He turns, teeth bared and nostrils flaring.

I raise the gun and shoot into the roof. Livvie shrieks, grabbing my arm. Jim jumps back with fear in his eyes, and Fern wails.

With buzzing ears, I cock the gun again and yell, "I've got six more of those. The next one goes to your roger." I point the gun just below his belt.

Sully's half out the door.

I examine the hole in the ceiling and sigh. Before heading out to look for Sully and Jim, Tucker took a look at the roof and said they can patch it up no problem.

Livvie sits with her arm wrapped around a very pregnant and frightened Fern.

I pull up a chair close and pat Fern's leg. "You can trust Lee. He's a real gentleman. You can stay the night with us, and he'll take you into town tomorrow. There's a good midwife there. Livvie's visited her."

Fern smiles weakly. "Thank you."

Livvie lays a hand on Fern's stomach. "Did you lose your husband?"

"I don't have a husband."

Livvie sighs and caresses her own belly. "Me either."

"Where's the child's father?" I ask.

The frosty snow pelts the house and a falling log thumps in the stove.

"You sent him out there." She points towards the door.

My brows furrow. "One of your brothers is the father?"

She shakes her head. "They're not my brothers." Her eyes are still downcast, and her back is slouched. "I don't know which of them is the father."

Livvie wraps another arm around the woman. "Oh, Fern."

I should have killed those sons of bitches when I had the chance.

"There was talk," Fern continues, "of two women who live alone up here. Jimmy said I'm such a horrible cook that they needed another woman. And Sully says he's sickened by my body and wishes for another until after the child's born."

They came for me and Livvie. I'm horrified by Fern's admission. That she's had to lay herself bare before those two repugnant men both saddens and disgusts me.

I peer back to the door for what feels like the hundredth time. It's still bolted shut.

18

Ginny

Livvie has put on a little extra weight. Baby weight, that is, as her belly has grown since she arrived. We joke that it's because the fellas feed us so well. Her sickness has passed as Mirna said it should, but I know her heart still aches as she cries herself to sleep most nights. And I'm sure the incident with Sully, Jim, and Fern frightened her enough that she's torn between leaving and not wishing me to be alone here.

Justus has been writing her, and I can't understand why she won't go back to him. I don't wish for her to leave me, but I want her to be happy. I want her to have the family I always dreamt of but shall never have now that Jake's gone. I know Mirna insists love will come, but Jake is the only love for me. I can't imagine my heart belonging to anyone else.

Finally, I'm able to convince Livvie to go to Laurel Springs.

She told me all about attempting to help her friend Rebecca find her family who was sold into slavery. She and Justus placed ads in newspapers out east in hopes that Rebecca's husband or the daughters she was separated from would read one of them. Alas, Justus's Aunt Bea wrote that Rebecca's husband has been found and is coming to Colorado, so they'll be having a party and insists Livvie attend. I know she's apprehensive due to her current condition, but I believe we can easily hide her expanding waistline with a large shawl I have in my trunk.

I reach under my bed and pull the handle of the case which hasn't been opened in years. Blowing the dust from the top, I unlatch it, and I'm taken back to the day Jake pushed it under the bed for me. I wonder if I'd have done or said anything different had I known he'd never again lay a hand on this chest.

Swallowing the lump in my throat, I sift through the items. Cloth which could be used to make clothing for the baby. Letters Jake and I wrote to one another while courting. I run my hand over his handwriting, proof he was alive once.

Livvie kneels beside me and rubs my back.

"It's just not fair." I continue to study every line and curve of his words.

"I know." She lays her head on my shoulder.

I swipe away a tear and tuck the missives back in the trunk. I must not allow myself to wallow in self-pity. Spotting the shawl I was looking for, I pull it free. "Here we are." It's a light brown, with accents of dark brown, knit shawl with fringe.

"Oh, Ginny, it's lovely." Livvie holds it up to examine the pattern. She stands and wraps it around herself. "This will be perfect."

I pull it together at her neck. "You can lace it or leave it open."

She ties the string at the collar. "I think I'll tie it. It will cover the front of me better and I won't risk it falling off." She smiles.

Livvie does a little twirl. "I can't believe you don't wear this."

I chuckle. "When and where would I don such a thing?"

She sighs. "Yes, certainly you don't wish to ruin it. But we must find an occasion for you to wear it."

I close the trunk and shove it back under my bed. "Well, for now it's yours to enjoy. I'm sure my mother-in-law would be delighted knowing it's getting use."

Laurel Springs is a lovely town nestled at the foot of the mountain range, and Miss Bea's family is even more lovely. They are so welcoming, I cannot understand how Livvie could leave these people.

Of course, I appreciate what Jake built for me, but I find myself giddy with excitement at the thought of sleeping in a sturdy home with a comfortable bed. Not to mention that this is the first time I've left the mountain since Jake and I came to Colorado from New York.

Livvie is so nervous she wrung her hands the entire trip here.

"Breathe," I'd remind her. "Everything's going to be all right."

I've had a sense that everything truly will be all right.

Miss Bea, Rebecca, Miss Bea's daughter Hannah, Livvie, and I are all in the kitchen preparing the supper meal. Miss Bea had said Justus was invited, but apparently no one knows if he will show himself or not.

"We haven't seen much of him since…" Miss Bea looks to Livvie and wipes her hands with her apron. "Anyway, he most likely won't come, I'm sorry to say."

My heart drops for my friend. I know even if she won't admit it to me, she hopes to see him.

We go about our work—Livvie taking plates from the cabinet, Rebecca fixing gravy, Miss Bea pulling pies from the oven, and I slicing bread—when a deep warm voice draws my attention from the task at hand.

"Well, hello, beautiful ladies."

"Justus." Miss Bea wraps him in a hug.

I spin around, eyebrows raised and a tight-lipped smile on my face, to see Livvie's reaction. This man is tall and *ruggedly handsome*, exactly as she'd described him. My stomach does flip flops for my friend.

Miss Bea holds her arm out towards me. "Justus, this is Olivia's friend Ginny."

He bows exaggeratedly and offers his hand. "Ginny, it's nice to meet you. I wish I'd heard all about you."

I glance at Livvie. I can't help myself and say, "Justus, it's nice to meet you. As a matter of fact, I *have* heard all about you." While shaking his hand.

He tips his head to Livvie. "Liv."

"Justus." She tips her head to him in reply but diverts her eyes elsewhere.

Inwardly, I'm so excited for these two I can hardly keep from busting open like a popcorn kernel.

At dinner it is quite clear they are both having a hard time being in the same room together. The tension is so thick it feels oppressive.

Miss Bea is speaking to Justus, but it's clear he's not truly present. "Justus? Are you all right, dear?"

Of course he's not all right. He appears mad. Perhaps it's sadness. I can't quite place his emotions. Maybe he's trying not to cry. I'm sure he feels that wouldn't be a manly thing to do.

"Actually, I need to go. I'm sorry." He rises from the table and turns to Rebecca. "I'm really happy for you, Rebecca, and I look forward to meeting your husband." He pushes in his chair. "Good night, everyone."

Livvie stands. "Justus."

Oh dear. I look from Justus to Livvie, then to the still faces around the table. There's a clank of a utensil against a plate.

"Justus, please stay." Livvie's trying not to cry. Before I know it, she's apologizing and taking off the shawl to show her growing belly.

My heart aches for her as I pull a handkerchief from my sleeve and hand it to her.

The events that follow happen so quickly that, before we know it, Justus is on bended knee, offering Livvie a ring he had specially made for her, and shortly thereafter, he leaves to fetch a man by the name of Silas. It seems that a wedding is taking place tonight.

So, it's certain I'll be returning home alone.

19

Silas

As usual, it's quiet at the McCalister table. I push green beans around on my plate, working up the nerve to speak. Perhaps instead of leaving town, I can step down as the pastor. I've considered speaking with the McCalisters about it, and as I'm working up the nerve to broach the subject, there's a rapid knock from the front door.

"Someone must be in trouble." Mister McCalister has a puzzled look about him. He sets his napkin on the table and goes to the front of the house. I'm unsure how a rapid knock at the door during supper means someone is in trouble. I shake my head at his statement. He's a curious fellow.

Voices carry, but I'm unable to make out the words, then Justus rushes into the dining room. "Silas, please. I need you to come to Doc and Miss Bea's." His hands are together in a prayer position.

I move my chair back from the table. "Justus, what's

happened?" Concern grabs my chest. Perhaps I judged Mister McCalister's thoughts too harshly.

"It's Olivia, she's here." He smiles, almost a giggle escapes. "I need you to come marry us, tonight. Please, Silas." He leans in and whispers to me. "We're having a baby."

I laugh. "Justus, what on earth?"

"Please." He looks down at my plate of food. "My aunt will feed you, I promise." He turns to the McCalisters, who are staring at him as though he's completely mad. "I'm so sorry about this sir, ma'am."

I shake my head. "Let me get my coat."

Justus pats my shoulder. "Thank you, brother." He has a grin from ear to ear, and I know he's not calling me brother in the brother in Christ sense of the word, but in the friends that we've become.

I tip my head to Missus McCalister. "Thank you for the lovely meal."

When we arrive at Doc and Miss Bea's, everyone is hustling about decorating the front room of the Peterson home. I'm surprised to see an unfamiliar young woman there. Clint obviously notices me noticing her, because he leans in and whispers, "That's Olivia's friend, Ginny. The woman whom she's been living with."

Ginny. I roll her name around in my mind. She looks like a Ginny. She's beautiful, with long blonde hair flowing down her back and a smile that causes my chest to do a little flip flop. I can't help but notice her fair skin and how the dress she wears sinches her waist and lifts her voluptuous, although completely covered, breasts. I'm feeling things I haven't felt in a very long time. She's more than looks, though, she's life. It's a feeling I couldn't explain if I tried. There's a light about her I've never known before. She truly shines.

Holding Miss Bea's scruffy old cat, Mister Harold, she hugs and kisses it—an act that both repulses and invigorates me— revealing to me that she loves animals, or at least cats.

"Thomas." Ginny holds the animal to her breast and strokes its head. "Will you put this chair over here for me?" She continues to pet the feline while kissing its head. I see wheels turning in her mind as she thinks of the next furniture placement for this impromptu wedding ceremony in the Peterson's sitting room.

Everything has happened so fast, we've not been formally introduced and to be honest, I don't believe she even knows I'm here.

"Perfect, Thomas," she says, still holding the cat in one arm while pulling the boy to her in the other. He beams. I would too if she hugged me. He's at the right height to be face to face with her chest. There certainly is something special about her, aside from her large breasts. She's only been here mere hours, and she fits right in. There's not a shy bone in her body, I'm sure of it.

"Oh, Ginny dear," Miss Bea calls as she bounds into the room. "Are we ready?"

"We certainly are. Thomas is such a great helper." She winks at the boy, and he grins. "I'll go fetch the bride. She won't come down until she hears the piano begin." Ginny swiftly leaves the room, still clutching that awful looking cat.

Now I need to focus on the reason I'm here, to wed Justus and Olivia.

20

Ginny

Livvie is stunning in the Chinese pagoda print dress Hannah leant her. I think of the dress I'm in, leant to me by Rebecca. I can't remember the last time I dressed up. Although a bit uncomfortable in this exceptionally snug gown, tied tightly at the back, I feel beautiful. Jake would think so. I can hear him now, *You're always beautiful.* His smile comes to mind. But of course he'd say that. Even when I'm wearing his trousers and have dirt on my face, he still thinks I'm beautiful. My chest tightens. He *thought* I was beautiful.

The wedding ceremony was almost as stunning as the bride, and Silas has a wonderful sense of humor for being a pastor.

As we sit at the dining table enjoying dessert to celebrate

the new couple, it occurs to me that Silas's wife isn't here. Don't preachers' wives attend everything? I lean into Livvie. "Shouldn't the pastor's wife be here?" I whisper.

"He doesn't have a wife," she whispers back.

"Oh, I guess that's a good reason, then."

How is this man not married? He has a most delightful wit and an undeniable charm, with strikingly handsome features— his hair a deep shade of brown, akin to the rich hue of coffee, and eyes as bright blue as the sky on a perfect, clear day. His clean-shaven face stands out, which is a rare sight for me as I'm more accustomed to the gruffy faces of the miners.

The thought of those fellas makes my heart clench. I love them more than they'll ever know.

t's true, a day may begin as any other, yet end like no other. The thought comes to me after we send Justus and Livvie off as husband and wife. And here I am, in a strange home with strange people, only none of it feels strange. It all feels so right and so natural. I already love these people.

Once everyone but Silas is gone, I turn to the preacher. "I'm curious, why do you insist on being called by your first name?"

He leans into me. "Because all my friends call me Silas."

"And what brought you to Laurel Springs? I hear you just arrived last summer."

"The seminary school I attended directed me here. Reverend Moore was leaving, and the Laurel Springs Church needed a pastor. I'm told they requested someone *young*." He smiles and waves to his face. His oh so handsome, smooth face. My fingers prickle at the desire to touch his strong jawline.

"And what made you decide to become a preacher? Is it something you dreamed of all your life?" I need to focus on something else to keep myself from getting lost in his gem-like eyes.

His smile fades. "No. And it's a long story."

It's obviously a story he doesn't wish to recount, and I respect that.

Thomas runs into the dining room. "Reverend Flynn, Ginny, can we play hide the thimble?"

"Why, I haven't played hide the thimble since I was about your age, Thomas," says Silas with eyes sparkling. He peers down at the table as if recalling a memory. "My brothers Jody, Paul, and I would play."

"You have brothers?" asks Thomas.

"Sure do. They're older than me." He glances around the table. "I believe they'd go easy on me because I was the baby. They'd pretend they hid the thimble real good but I'd find it quick and they'd say, 'Why, Silas, you're the best thimble finder.'" He chuckles, and I see a sweet vulnerability in him that warms my heart.

I surprise myself by blurting, "Well, we'll see just how good you are, Preacher, once we get the dishes washed and put away."

When he glances at me, my stomach flutters at the twinkle in his eyes. Amusement plays on his face, and I feel caught off guard by the vibrations running through my body as we share a lingering gaze.

I hear a voice, *He's the one.* No. It's only my head thinking up something ridiculous, we've only just met.

Silas grins. "I suppose I better roll up my sleeves." Then he stands and begins grabbing dishes from the table.

When I rise, my breath hitches and I lose my balance, slightly falling towards him.

"Woah," he says with a laugh, grabbing my arm to steady me. I feel the strength of his grasp, and I find myself yearning to wrap my arms around him. It's been so long since I've felt the strong embrace of a man that I forgot how wonderful it feels. I push past the thickness in my throat as I swallow.

"I apologize. I suppose I stood too fast." A tingle glides up my neck and across my face.

"I'd say so. Do you need to sit back down?"

I realize he's still holding dishes in one hand.

"No, thank you. I'll be fine."

He truly is a gentleman, and I'm foolish for entertaining any thoughts other than regarding him as a kind and respectable preacher.

Silas tosses the thimble back and forth from one hand to the other. They're rough and calloused from hard work. I'm accustomed to seeing hands like these but surprised to see them on him and wonder what he does aside from preaching.

"All right, Thomas, here's the rules. We'll wait here in the sitting room until you're ready for us to come out." Silas holds the thimble up. "You can't hide this upstairs, in a closet, cupboard, drawer, or behind anything."

The boy nods. "I know the rules."

Silas laughs and tosses the silver piece into the air. Thomas catches it and runs off down the hall to the kitchen.

A few moments later we hear him shout, "I'm ready."

When Miss Bea, Rebecca, Silas, and I enter the kitchen, I immediately see it. It's perched on the windowsill above the sink, so I head in the opposite direction peering around the room pretending as though I haven't a clue. "Hmmm, where is it?" I ponder aloud.

"You're really cold, Ginny. *Freezing*," says a giggling Thomas.

I turn and realize Silas has noticed it too. He gives me a wink and my stomach flutters.

Silas rubs his chin. "You've done well, young man. You've got me stumped."

Thomas grins behind little brown fingers.

Rebecca glances about as she makes her way closer to the sink.

"You're burnin' up, Mama." His eyes are big and round with excitement.

"Am I now?" Pausing, she plucks the thimble from the window. "Aha!" She twists towards Thomas. "I guess it's my turn to hide it now."

"It is," he shouts and runs down the hall to the sitting room.

I'm proud of my own hiding skills and have been hard to beat over a few rounds of the game, but Silas finds the thimble now, which means it's finally his first turn.

When we enter the dining room, I spot him out of the corner of my eye, leaning back against the wall with his arms folded and one foot crossed over the other.

Rebecca, Thomas, Miss Bea, and I are all diligently scanning the pictures on the walls, the chairs, under the table, and around Miss Bea's hutch. When I pop my head up from under the table a second time, I look at the man in exasperation. He's grinning like a cheshire cat, ear to ear.

With my hands on my hips, I study him. "Where could you have put that thing?" I ask.

He raises an eyebrow, and I feel like I'm melting to the spot. I imagine how sliding my fingers through his hair must feel, what his lips must be like to kiss, his strong jaw, wrapping my arms around his neck and sliding them down his...*what*? I stomp my foot, march over to him, and snatch up the thimble that is balancing on his shoulder.

"You all," I say to the others, "This man had it sitting on his *shoulder*."

Silas smacks his hands together in a burst of laughter.

Miss Bea snaps her fingers. "Well, I'll be. I hadn't even thought of giving you one look, Silas."

I feel heat rise in my cheeks as I was doing more than merely *looking* at the man. I was positively daydreaming about him.

Rebecca smooths her hand over Thomas's head. "It's getting late, but what do we think about having some popcorn before retiring for the night?"

Thomas turns to Silas with a partially toothy grin. "Will you stay and have popcorn with us?"

Silas glances at me before giving his attention to Thomas. "I love popcorn. Come on. Let's see what we can do to help your mama."

I watch them as they leave the room, and I ponder the glances between me and Silas. I smile as fluttering fills my insides.

Remembering Jake, I straighten. It's not right for me to flirt with a man who is not my husband. Besides, Silas wouldn't be so coy if he knew I'm not a Christian. I admonish myself and head for the kitchen. I'll be returning home tomorrow anyhow.

21

Ginny

It's a breathtaking day, gliding through the mountains with Justus and Livvie in their sleigh, with the backseat all to myself. They're escorting me back to my home, and while there, they'll be collecting Livvie's belongings. I'll miss her sorely.

We spend the couple hours of travel it takes to discuss the previous day's activities. I still can't believe Justus and Livvie are married, and Livvie still can't believe Silas played hide the thimble with us. This has also been a wonderful time of getting to know Justus and feeling confident I'm leaving my friend in good hands. Life won't be the same without her, but I've promised to take a stagecoach in the summer after she delivers the baby so he or she can meet their Aunt Ginny. An idea Livvie is thrilled with.

My thoughts turn to my furry buddy at home. "I wonder how Buck's fared without me. I sure miss him." I can't wait to see him and cuddle him. We've never been apart one day in close to four years.

"He's probably lying at the door waiting for you," Livvie says. I'm sure she's right.

As we round the bend, my heart and stomach drop. My home is in a smoldering heap, and the men are standing around it with buckets. Soot streaks their faces. A scream escapes me, and I attempt to jump from the sleigh just as it comes to an abrupt halt. "No, no, no!" I shout.

"We were too late, Ginny," says one of the men. My mind is unable to process which one. "We're so sorry."

I fall into Livvie's arms. It's as if I'm experiencing the heartbreak of Jake's loss anew. I'm reminded of sobbing into Big Joe's chest when we buried my husband. Tears overwhelm me once more, shaking me to my core. Livvie and I fall to the ground and cry together. Justus takes us both into his arms and holds us, letting the tears fall.

Oh, no, Buck! I jump to my feet and turn towards the men. "Where's Buck? Where's Buck?" My hands fly to my face in terror as I frantically search the rubble.

Tucker shakes his head, his face black with smoke residue. "I haven't seen him."

"Oh no!" I'm frantic as I run around what's left of my home, crying for my companion, scared that somehow he's in this ash heap. "I need Buck."

"Ginny! Ginny, he's here," Livvie calls to me, and I run to her.

I can't get to my four-legged friend quick enough. "Oh Buck, I thought I'd gone and lost you, too. Why'd you scare me like that?" Giggles bubble as Buck licks the tears from my face. I thought he was gone forever, and I couldn't bear such a thing.

After a moment, my thumping heart returns to normal and I sit in disbelief on a stump beside Livvie, petting my sweet boy who sleeps in my lap. "I don't know what I'm going to do, Livvie. I've lost everything. And you…" My heart fractures into pieces as I gaze upon my friend. "You've lost everything, too. I'm so sorry. I feel as though somehow it's my fault. I should have stayed behind."

"Although my heart aches for my only worldly possessions, including my grandparents' letters and my grandmother's ring, I know I haven't lost everything. I gained more than I could ask or hope for—a family. It's a small fortune, but I feel as rich in wealth as the Queen of England." Livvie wraps an arm around me and pulls me close. "I've got you, my friend, and for that, I'm so thankful. What if you'd stayed and had been in there?"'

"Oh, I would've gotten out," I say it with the utmost confidence.

"But what if you hadn't?"

Justus bends down beside us. "Rumor has it that some men who didn't take too kindly to you ladies turning down their advances did this. I'm thankful you weren't here. Who knows what they would have done to you."

My stomach tightens as I recall Fern confessing Sully and Jim wished to take me and Livvie as wives. Livvie's right, it's a good thing I wasn't home.

Just when I believe I have no choice this time but to return to New York, Justus and Livvie convince me to go back to Laurel Springs with them.

"Trust me," says Justus. "My aunt would be over the moon if you stayed with them."

Jake. Oh, Jake. I'll have to leave him behind and a new wave of nausea rushes over me. "I have one thing I need to do before we go," I say. "I have to tell Jake goodbye." Buck follows as I slowly make my way to Jake's gravesite.

I kneel at the pile of rocks, covered in the snow from the previous night's storm, that protect my husband's body from predators. Laying my own body across them, I succumb to sobbing once more. "I'm so sorry, Jake. I'm so sorry." I repeat it again and again, and with each utterance, a gentle warmth seems to envelop me, as though I were being embraced in a tender hug.

It's all right Virginia, he says softly. *Wherever you go, I'll be there. My body is here, yes, but my spirit is free. Always remember.*

My hand covers my chest where the little lavender stone is tucked away under my blouse.

"But this land. I could rebuild." We only have another year, and the claim will be completely ours. I was concerned when Jake died that the government would take it from me because I'm a woman, but the kind man at the land office in Sutton's Creek told me because I'm Jake's wife it would transfer to me.

I sense Jake's smile. *Go back with Justus and Livvie to Laurel Springs, that's where you belong now.*

I ache inside in ways I couldn't explain if I tried. Jake is gone, our home is gone, and now the land shall be gone. If only I could at least sell it. This life is hell. Hades is right here on earth. Mirna is right. *Oh, Mirna!* I won't even get the opportunity to see her and say goodbye. I'll have to find my way back in the spring, until then I'll write to her. Oh, how I'll miss my dear friend.

I'm numb. Not because of the cold, but because I feel empty

inside, like a shell of a body moving with no meaning or purpose.

Come on, Ginny, it's time you head back. It's almost as if Jake's lifting me from this spot, moving one foot in front of the other for me. For him, I'll make the most of whatever life has for me.

22

Silas

As I step back from the barn doors, the scent of hay drifts toward me, and I gesture for Rebecca's husband, Samuel, to go on in. Everyone, including Rebecca and their son, Thomas, whom Samuel has yet to learn about, wait inside.

The whole scene that unfolds before us is emotional and special beyond words. There are many tears as the family is reunited and Samuel and Thomas meet for the first time.

Samuel, who had fallen to a knee to embrace his son, rises, wipes his face with a handkerchief he's pulled from his pocket, then surveys the faces of the strangers. "I s'pose I'll get to learning who the rest of you are as the night goes on." He opens his arms wide. "Shall we celebrate?"

"Here, here," says Frank as he takes his fiddle from the box and begins to play.

Justus and Livvie have transformed the barn into a lovely

space for a family to reunite and friends to celebrate. Bales of hay make up seating, beams are draped in greenery, lanterns hang from posts, and tables are lined with an array of food.

I'm greeted by church folk as I search the crowd for Ginny. Once spotted, I make my way towards her, rubbing my hands together. *I'm a single man and she's a single woman. We should be able to dance with the rest, shouldn't we?*

She stands by a table with Livvie, inspecting the collection of pies spread across its surface. Ginny is a sight to behold with curves that have me all tied up inside. Her blonde locks are swept up off her neck, and I wonder how it would be to kiss that tender, exposed skin just below her ear. The dress she's wearing matches the color of her icy blue eyes.

"I think he wants mincemeat," I hear Livvie state.

A smile plays on my lips.

"Awful." Ginny swats the air. "Worst pie ever."

I can't help but add, "I agree." It is awful and I'm happy to learn we have something in common, besides the enjoyment of playing hide the thimble.

Ginny straightens and looks away. I don't understand her nervous reaction since we had such a grand time at Doc and Miss Bea's the other night. I have felt terrible since learning about her home, but I must admit I'm happy that I'll get to see more of her. It's selfish I know, and I've internally chided myself for the thought many times over since hearing the news.

"I hear you're going to be making Laurel Springs your home now," I say.

"Yes, Miss Bea and Doc have offered me a room in their home."

"I'm happy to learn you'll be staying. It'll be nice seeing you around."

She bites her lip and glances at the floor.

Frank begins a new song on his fiddle, and I hold out my hand to her. "May I have this dance?"

"I'm afraid I'm not very good." She peeks towards Livvie.

I'm unsure if she's hoping her friend will save her from me or if she's only nervous. Doubtful.

I find her claims hard to believe so I press, "That's all right. Just follow my lead," I exclaim, my hand still extended. I'm beginning to feel like a fool behind my wavering smile.

She sways as if giving this thought. "You won't laugh if I fall on my face?"

I chuckle. "Not too hard."

She briefly glimpses Livvie, who's thoroughly enjoying her dessert. "Well, all right," she concedes and takes my hand.

Once on the dance floor, I learn this woman knows exactly what she is doing. There's no need for me to lead her anywhere. My desire for her runs so deep, I don't believe I could ever reach its core, even if I spent a lifetime searching. Her eyes soften and her lips part. A warmth washes over me, and a slow smile builds across my face. She returns the expression and it's as if we're the only two people in the room.

When the music stops, we reluctantly part.

I tip my head towards her. "I hope to have the pleasure of another dance with you before the night ends."

With her hands clasped behind her back she lowers her gaze. "Perhaps."

I gesture away from the dance floor toward Livvie, who is sitting and conversing with her friend Lenny Johnson.

Before I can step away, a couple of young ladies behind Ginny giggle while asking me to dance. Although I only have eyes for one, I believe it wouldn't be prudent if I show favoritism towards Ginny alone, so I concede.

"Oh, but who do I dance with first?"

They giggle again and one points to the other. "You can go first."

I'm sure I'm not a very good dance partner as I spend my time searching the room for Ginny, who does not, I note, dance with any other men. A few times I've noticed her watching me, but she quickly glances away as if she were caught doing something she shouldn't. I smile inside at the jealousy I feel emanating from her.

Oh, Ginny, what am I going to do with you?

Already, what I've learned of this woman makes me appreciate her, and I yearn to spend more time in her presence. How I can make that happen, I'm unsure, but I must find a way.

23

Ginny

Lenny Johnson's tailor shop is larger than I anticipated. There's a parlor stove with a flat top, a couch, a chair, and a lot of clothing. Some folded neatly on a table and some hung. There are a few garments draped over the sofa. Lenny stands sipping coffee while looking out the back window onto the street behind her store.

At Rebecca's party the other night, where we became instant friends, she invited me to come by to discuss partnering. Livvie had told her about my laundress business and Lenny thought it might be a good addition to her seamstress shop.

She doesn't turn to me when I enter and shut the door. I watch her, unsure of what to say. I suppose good morning would be appropriate, but I guess I'm expecting her to notice me first. I feel slightly uneasy, being unnoticed. Perhaps she forgot she'd offered for me to come by.

"How many of those men out there this morning do you suppose are unfaithful to their wives?" she asks, still glaring out the window.

Her question takes me by surprise. "What do you mean?" I inch towards her to look out the panes of glass. Maybe she's referring to something specific.

"These men, supposedly going to work or the feed store or the mercantile. How many do you believe are faithful to their wives?"

I peer through the window. "I've never thought about it, I suppose."

A hush falls over us before my words fill the air once more. "I guess I tend to believe when a man marries, it's for love."

I turn to her. "What's this truly about?" I know Lenny services men in the evenings and that she fell in love with one of them—Jesse is his name, if I recall correctly. She hasn't seen or heard from him in months. I can feel the woman's pain flowing from her.

There's more to him than she knows. I place my hand over my stone to still my thoughts.

"It's possible for them to love their wives and still be unfaithful. Men are carnal beings. They need the feel and scent of a woman." Her finger moves around the rim of her cup.

Laying her head against the window she stares at me. "My papa used to tell me the only way I'd ever keep a man was to please him in bed."

"Oh, Lenny." I lay my head against the glass, mimicking her posture. *What a terrible thing for a father to say to his daughter. What kind of man would do that?*

She smiles and shifts her eyes out onto the street. "It's ironic. I've done my best, but no one's ever stayed."

I run my hand down her arm. "Your papa was wrong. There's more to relationships than that. You must be able to make each other laugh, give more than you take, and be there even when you don't feel like it. You must respect one another." I grin. "If the love making is good, well, that's but icing on the already velvety cake."

She smiles back and straightens herself.

Folding my arms, I take a step away. "Personally, I wouldn't wish to be with a man who wasn't good in bed, but I'll be damned if that's reason enough to keep him."

Lenny closes her eyes and pivots on her feet towards the woodstove. "Oh, I apologize, Ginny. I've said too much."

She pours coffee in a cup and hands it to me. "You must think I'm something terrible."

"No. I think you're a woman who finds men to be exasperating, like the rest of us."

She motions for me to have a seat on the sofa. "Livvie said your husband passed some years ago, I'm sorry."

I nod. "Yes, and apparently it's time for me to move on."

"Who says?"

"Since it appears this is confessional time, I'll tell you as I know you won't judge me anymore than I'd ever judge you."

"Come now, do tell." Lenny flips her hand in the air. "I love a good confession." She narrows her eyes at me. "Is this going to send you straight to hell?"

I chuckle. "If I believed in the place, yes."

"I just knew we'd be good friends." Lenny sips her coffee while giving me that *I'm listening* look.

"Since Jake died, I've had a knowing about things."

Lenny leans forward with eyes the size of saucers. "Are you one of those fortune tellers?"

I shake my head and laugh. "Nooo. I am not a fortune teller either. I just know things and I can't explain it. I feel things and I hear things. I'm sure some would say I'm of the devil, but I can promise I'm of no such thing."

"So, what do you know? Can you tell me my future?"

"I'm sorry, I know nothing of your future." I give her a half smile.

"What kind of knower are you then?" Lenny says it as if I'm useless.

"I can't tell you. All I can say is I can hear, not like I can hear you, but I can hear when Jake, my husband, speaks to me. And I can feel him."

"Huh," Lenny sounds as if to say *imagine that*. "What else do you got?"

I take a drink of my coffee. "What do you mean?"

She lounges back in her chair. "I'm a bit of a knower myself, and I know that's not your greatest sin." She puts her fist to her chest. "I can *feel* it."

I sigh. "I was *nearly* intimate with another man after Jake died."

"Go on."

"He was a friend. I was angry, sad, confused."

Lenny raises an eyebrow. "How nearly did you get?"

I stare into my cup. The liquid is as black as tar. The woman makes terrible coffee. "We were in my bed and bare as the day we were born." I smirk.

"What happened?"

"I stopped it before it got too far. He wished for marriage, but that wouldn't have been fair to either of us."

"Have you considered the possibility of remarrying in the future?"

I smile and stretch an arm out in front of me. "I'm told there's a love for me, so perhaps." I bat my eyes.

"Is there someone you have in mind? Perhaps that preacher man?" Lenny says in a sly tone.

"Because we danced? Oh no. I could never be a preacher's wife."

I'm certain Silas is fond of me, because while dancing with others, he continued to glance my way. And at church whenever he notices me, he seems to forget what he's saying.

"I saw the way he was looking at you. He didn't give the other ladies he danced with those smoldering eyes." She shrugs with a lift of her brows as if to say *you never know.* "He's spellbound by your beauty," she purrs.

I laugh. "Well, it can never be. I'm not a church goer."

"Oh yes you are. As long as you live under the Peterson roof you are."

"You know what I mean, Lenny. I could never be with a preacher. Can you even imagine?" My face cringes.

"He's probably a virgin," she suggests, examining her nails. "You could send him to me. I can teach him a thing or two for you."

I gasp. "You're terrible."

"It's not the first time I've heard that."

"Thank you," I say, wishing to change the subject. "For

offering me the position of laundress here at your shop."

"Well, Livvie went and got herself in the family way and married that beautiful cowboy, so I don't have much choice." She winks and gently pushes my knee.

"I know. Can you believe she left me for that man?" I sip my coffee. "It's a good thing my cabin burned down and forced me to move here to Laurel Springs," I joke. "Otherwise I'd be completely alone."

"It truly is." Her stare is far away. "Well, you've saved me. Thank you," she adds, snapping out of her trance. "And I plan to add *Laundry* to the sign out front." She moves her hands over her head as if she's envisioning this new sign.

Two things are now certain in my life. One, I have a job working alongside a new friend. And two, I shall not be courting the town's preacher.

24

Silas

"Let us pray, shall we." I peer out into the faces of the church folk. I've managed to preach on another topic I can safely speak about. Loving thy neighbor.

As the congregation departs, I notice Mister McCalister and the other men from the church board remain behind. I tug at the collar of my shirt. Once the room has emptied, Robert Simpson clears his throat and steps forward. My hope is that I said something during the service they don't agree with and not the truth that I fear.

"Reverend Flynn, please have a seat." The large man motions for me to sit in a pew.

"I'd prefer to stand, thank you." I'm not going to allow him to chastise me while hovering over me as if I were a child.

He rocks on his feet, back to front. "We have reason to believe, from a reputable source, that you were dancing at a gathering held at the Bennett Ranch on Monday evening."

Ah, there it is. And reputable? I'm certain it was Bridget Murphy, the only daughter to the town banker. That sly girl has a way of causing trouble at every opportunity. I heard all about the strife she created for Justus last year attempting to rope him into marriage. And when Livvie's so-called brother-in-law who was set on having her for a wife came to town to claim her, Bridget told him where to find her. The awful man ended up killing a lawman before being taken back to Missouri and hung for his crime.

I cock my head as anger stirs in me. Anger at Bridget Murphy and anger at these men for their hypocrisy. I am aware that Robert Simpson has behaved in a most abusive manner towards his wife. I'm also aware that these men put more tithing money in their pockets than they do into the church while telling their congregation it's a sin to not give a tenth every week. Many of the church folk don't know where their next meal will come from. And I observed with my own two eyes Joseph Perry strike his child across the head and tell him he was ignorant. I'm beginning to wonder if God, the true God, not the one these men worship, condones this behavior.

"Did David not dance before the Lord?" I ask, my tone steady but serious. My heart is running with anger at their accusation against me as if dancing is improper.

"I'd be careful if I were you, Reverend," warns Milton Brady. "You know full well dancing with a woman leads to lustful thoughts, and lustful thoughts leads to lustful acts." He turns towards the other men and raises his voice. "And we've been told you danced with *several* women."

Mister McCalister steps forward, a timid man fumbling with his hat. "The town loves you, Reverend, and we'd hate to have to let you go." He glances to the other men. "I believe we can all agree this is a warning. We can't have that kind of behavior from our minister. It doesn't look proper."

I square my shoulders. I won't permit these men to see me appear weak or defeated. "I understand. No dancing."

In all reality this is my way out. Them letting me go would be the best thing I could grant them to do. But on principle alone, I won't be moved.

"Well now," Brady quips. "I'm glad we have an understanding."

By the time they exit the building, I'm shaking. I sit in a pew and stare at the front of the room studying the pulpit, the piano, and the cross that looms on the wall. Why did I allow myself to get into this mess? I know what I've done is wrong, and I know I'm way in over my head. The war waging within me between wanting to leave this town and not wanting to leave ensues.

If only these people knew where I've come from and what I've done, they'd surely cast me out, condemning me to the eternal flames of perdition where there's weeping and gnashing of teeth, far more cruel than the mental prison I've trapped myself in.

I can't help but wonder if everything I was raised to believe is true, or if it's man's way of keeping us all compliant. What better way to get people to do what you wish than through fear. That's what my own father did to me. If I didn't obey, I was sure to feel his leather strap along my backside. I've even received a twist of the ear, flicks on the head, and twists of the arm. All of this, in addition to the ceaseless labor and being subjected to the vilest names, led me to believe I was destined to be a person of no consequence. I was thought to be lazy, unattractive, weak, and utterly pathetic.

If God is anything like my own father, then it's possible these men are right. If I dance with a woman, it will lead to lustful thoughts that will lead to lustful conduct that will lead me straight to a place of torment. And if I'm showing unbecoming behavior, it could cause others to believe that's permissible and they'll do it too. Before I know it, I've led innocent people to the depths of hell. According to their beliefs, that is.

Tucking my Bible under my arm, I lock the front of the church and leave out the back door to the parsonage. A smile forms on my face as my mind recalls twirling about Justus's barn with Ginny in my embrace. How can that which is so improper bring such pleasure? I believe dancing with that stunning woman is the most beautiful, natural, and right thing possible. It's possible God himself sent her to me. I grin so big a chuckle escapes my lips as I eagerly look forward to our next reunion.

25

Ginny

From Livvie's sunny new kitchen here on the Bennett Ranch, she kneads one batch of dough, while I attend to the other batch. It has been several weeks since I took up residence in Laurel Springs, and, wishing to allow the newlyweds their well-deserved honeymoon period, this is my first visit to the ranch since Rebecca and Samuel's reunion celebration. I have missed my dear friend sorely.

"How are you faring, living here and staying with Miss Bea?" Livvie folds the dough and punches it down with the balls of her hands.

"Everyone has been wonderful. Of course, I miss the fellas and Mirna. And, although I miss our bedtime discussions, I'm thankful I still have you close. I miss times like these when we work side by side." The dough is smooth and elastic in my palms. "Lenny has become a great companion in this short period of time as well."

Livvie chuckles. "I could see at the party that Lenny took right to you. I told her you were no different than she and I and she said, 'If she's a friend of yours, then she's a friend of mine.'"

This fills my heart with joy and brings a smile to my lips.

"I sure miss Buck something terrible." I stop and glance out the window knowing he's lazing on the porch. "I am so grateful to you and Justus for taking him in."

Livvie rights herself and swipes a strand of hair from her brow with the back of her hand. "Oh heavens, it's quite all right. He's a good dog, and we love having him. I believe Justus is going to be sad when the day comes for you to take him away. He gives that animal more attention than he gives me."

I laugh, well aware that she's merely jesting.

Livvie covers our bowls of dough with a linen cloth then wipes her hands on her apron. "Potatoes or carrots?"

"Carrots."

She and I always shared daily tasks when we lived together at my cabin. Instead of asking 'What would you like to do?' we'd offer two options, and whichever one I took, she'd take the other. It was our way—simple and unspoken, like so many things between us.

Even though we are in her kitchen now, it feels familiar.

"Has Silas been to Doc and Miss Bea's since hiding the thimble?" Livvie questions with a mischievous grin.

"Now why would you be asking about the preacher? You're a married woman." I lean forward. "Who doesn't even attend services, I might add."

"I saw how he noticed you. Even when he was dancing with

the other ladies, his attention was on a certain Virginia Price."

"You stop that, Olivia Bennett." I wag my head. She's reading more into things than is necessary. Although, I must admit it's the only good part about having to attend church.

Livvie leans forward gently placing her hand, still holding the knife, on the table. "It's all right for you to move on Ginny."

"I'm not ready." I keep my focus on slicing carrots.

"Honey, it's been well over three years. It's all right if you're not ready, but if you're resisting because you fear you're being unfaithful to Jake, then you're doing it for the wrong reason."

I put my hands in my lap and lean back. "He was my first love. The only love I've ever known."

"I know. But Ginny, he's not coming back. You said yourself he wished for you to move on and be happy. Mirna assured you that your heart would find its match once more, and that Jake gives his blessing."

I take our bowl of vegetables to the boiling pot on the stove and dump them in. "I don't know, Livvie."

She gives my arms a squeeze from behind. "Good news. You can take all the time you need. I just don't want you missing out, that's all. Also, I'm your friend, and as you encouraged me not to give up on Justus, it's my duty to encourage you to not give up on love for yourself."

"Well, if or when I may ever be ready, I can assure you it won't be with Silas Flynn. He's a preacher, for heaven's sake. Could you imagine me, a preacher's wife, mixing herbs in our kitchen or honoring the moon in the backyard of the parsonage?"

Livvie laughs. "You make a valid point."

Livvie and I have just finished setting the table when Justus walks in through the kitchen door leading to the outside. "Do you mind setting another place at the table?"

As the last word leaves his mouth, Silas appears behind him.

Livvie turns to me with a sly grin. "Why, it's Silas. Come on in."

Did she plan this, I wonder.

He removes his jacket, hanging it on the hook beside Justus's coat. "I'm sorry for intruding. I came out to see Justus about some land and he insisted I stay to eat."

Silas stops short when he notices me. "Ginny. Hello."

I nod. "Silas. It's good to see you, outside of church." My heart, my mind, and my stomach are doing funny things. All too familiar things. These are dangerous feelings to have about a preacher. A man you can't have even if you wanted him. *And I most definitely do not want him.*

During dinner, however, we can't seem to stop stealing glances at one another. I peep at Livvie and Justus who don't seem to notice. If they do, they aren't letting on that they do.

Everyone's attention moves to Livvie when she clears her throat. "I've decided since putting an ad in the papers out East helped us find Samuel, I'd like to give it another try to see if we can't still find his and Rebecca's daughters."

Poor Rebecca. There's a deep sorrow in me for what she and Samuel have been through.

Livvie continues. "I spoke with Rebecca regarding the matter, and she assured me she wouldn't oppose it."

Justus sops up gravy with a hunk of bread. "I believe that's a wonderful idea, Angel. Samuel has been a real asset here on the ranch. I'm happy they've reunited, and they deserve to be the family they were always meant to be." His eyes twinkle at his bride.

"I'm still greatly troubled by the events that took place in town last week," he adds.

Silas gives a puzzled look. "What happened?"

"I sent Samuel to town for feed, but Milton Brady refused to sell him any. Said he wouldn't serve him." Justus shakes his head in disgust. "Samuel told him he was there to pick it up for me, and Brady said I could come fetch it myself. So, I went on in there and told ole Brady that if he refused to sell Samuel feed then I'd take my business elsewhere, even if it meant traveling 50 miles."

Silas rocks his head back and forth in disbelief. "What did he say to that?"

"Oh, he knows I'm his most valued customer, so he was stammering over his words, stating he didn't know Samuel was there on my behalf. I made it clear I knew he was being dishonest and that this was his warning: should it occur again, he'd lose my business."

Silas sits back. "You know he's on the church board."

"I do." Justus swipes his napkin over his mouth.

Silas's lips tighten as in thought. "I don't believe it would be prudent of me to speak further on this. Ginny doesn't need the burden of knowing town gossip and ruining her thoughts on the church." He looks up at me. "My apologies."

Livvie, knowing I care none about the church, speaks up. "It's all right, Silas, you can speak frankly in front of Ginny."

He sighs and sets his fork down, harder than he means to, I'm sure. "Milton Brady and the rest of the church board cornered me after morning service the Sunday following Samuel and Rebecca's party and reprimanded me for dancing."

Livvie laughs. "Why, everyone was dancing." She glances around the table with a bewildered look.

Justus sets his cup down. "But Silas is the preacher. He's not permitted to have any joy. Joy leads to the eternal lake of fire."

Not understanding how Silas can put up with that, I can't help but ask, "What are you planning to do?"

He raises his brows and gives a half smile. "I have to obey the church board."

Livvie huffs. "Obey. That word makes me *ill*."

How can this grown man allow other men to treat him so? "It upsets me as well," I affirm. "I heard that word, obey, more than I cared for as a child. When I *disobeyed* my mother by marrying Jake and moving here, I felt liberated." I stare Silas in the eye. "You should try it."

He glares back and it's as if we're the only two people at this table.

26

Silas

Peering out the window with my hot cup of coffee in hand, I moan at the prospect of heading outdoors to shovel. March brought us a snowstorm in the night that weighs down every tree limb I spot. The morning sun glistens off each unique flake which is positively magical.

Drinking down the last of the steamy cup of liquid warmth, I layer on clothing and step out into the white powder. I soon find myself sweating as the air isn't as cold as I anticipated, and I remove layers of garments.

Once I have the parsonage and church shoveled and start back for the house, I'm surprised to see the McCalisters walkway and porch are still covered in the heavy wet snow, so I conclude the neighborly thing to do is to clear their path as well.

As I finish up, Missus McCalister pokes her head out, still wearing her night coat and a cap. "Reverend Flynn, I'm afraid both Mister McCalister and myself have caught a slight chill. Would you mind letting Miss Bea know I won't be making the sewing circle today?"

"Yes, of course. Is there anything I can do? Other than sending word to Miss Bea, that is? Should I fetch Doc as well? I'm sure that will be her first thought." I take a step back, not wanting to catch whatever the couple might have, although I may already have it considering I ate dinner with them yesterday evening.

"No. I'm able to take care of the two of us just fine." She nods to the porch. "Thank you for shoveling. It's appreciated." She gives a weary smile and goes back into the house.

As I raise my hand to knock on the door of the Peterson home, it flings open and Thomas barrels out, holding a large metal bowl, then stops abruptly when he notices me. "I apologize, Silas." He's doing his best to be courteous but simultaneously fidgeting with excitement. "How are you, sir?"

I must refrain from laughing. "Well, hello, Thomas. I wasn't expecting to see you here. And where are you off to with that bowl?"

"My ma let me come and play with Ginny yesterday, but because of the storm I ended up staying the night." He lifts the bowl. "We're going to make ice cream. I've never had it, but it sounds good."

Ginny steps out onto the porch. "Were you all raised in a barn? You're letting the cold in." She closes the door behind her then looks at me and winks causing my insides to turn to warm taffy.

Thomas runs off down the steps. "Be right back," he hollers.

"Play with Ginny?" I tilt my head to her.

She gives me a light slug to the arm. "I'm fun."

I grab my arm and wince as if she's hurt me, which makes her giggle.

"To what do we owe the pleasure of Reverend Silas Flynn paying us a visit?" She crosses her arms and smiles flirtatiously at me. *Is* she flirting with me?

"The McCalisters have caught a chill it seems. Missus McCalister asked that I inform Miss Bea that she will not be attending the sewing circle today."

Ginny rolls her eyes. "You mean the gossip circle," she whispers.

I cough back a laugh.

Thomas returns to the porch with his bowl heaping with snow. "Ready."

Ginny waves to me. "Come in. You can tell Miss Bea yourself before you help us make ice cream."

If she were any other woman, I'd believe she's a bit too friendly and forward with the preacher. But she's Ginny. And I'm not any ole preacher.

Miss Bea insists she and Doc go check up on the McCalisters, and I'm left standing in the kitchen with Ginny and Thomas to make this icy dessert. I'd heard of ice cream, but I've never tasted it.

"All right, Thomas, sweetheart," sings Ginny as she ties her apron on. "Let's take half of the snow and put it in this container so we can make two batches."

Thomas does as he's told while Ginny brings other ingredients from the pantry.

"Silas, you can mix one portion, and Thomas, you can mix the other."

She sets to pouring sugar and vanilla into two brass cups filled with milk before pouring them into our individual bowls of snow.

Thomas and I agree this doesn't seem right and that perhaps we need more cream for our *cream*.

"Oh, hush now and keep mixing," she chides while stirring caramel sauce at the stove.

She then sets it aside and gives each of our portions another good mix until she appears satisfied with the results.

"Thomas, sweetheart, grab us each a bowl and a spoon please."

I'm impressed at how lovely these desserts appear as she scoops nice little mounds of the cream into the dishes and drizzles them with the caramel.

I wish desperately to know this woman. I watch her every move, her slender fingers, her smile that makes me grin, her eyes that shine blue. She glances at me, and I clear my throat.

"I hear you're working at Lenny Johnson's."

Her eyes sparkle. "News travels fast, I see."

I shrug.

"I had a laundress business in Sutton's Creek, and Lenny thought it would be a good addition to the tailor shop. It's hard work, but I enjoy it. And I take great pride in a good, laundered shirt." She winks and hands a serving of ice cream to Thomas. "You get the first taste."

Thomas's eyes grow as big as saucers when he takes a spoonful. "Mmm, Ginny, this is delightful."

We laugh at his use of the word delightful as he digs his spoon back into the dish.

Ginny nudges his arm. "You had better go sit at the table with that, mister."

I take a bite, and the explosion of sweet flavors, mingled with the refreshing chill, fills my mouth with great satisfaction. "I have to agree with you, Thomas, this is quite…" I lean into Ginny who stands at my side, about to sample the dessert. "*Delightful.*"

She giggles and a drizzle of sauce travels down her lip onto her chin. I reach over and wipe it away with my thumb before realizing how inappropriate it was for me to do that. Ginny smiles and licks the spot my thumb had just been. Her gaze locks onto mine, and a shiver makes its way up my arms and into my chest. Remembering Thomas, I quickly glance at the boy, who's too busy eating to notice us. I suck the caramel from my thumb, aching to touch the woman beside me.

Gliding my spoon through the creamy goodness, I sneak a peek back to Ginny who I find studying me. She bites her bottom lip and my pulse quickens.

If dancing with her was a jewel, the way she looks at me is the whole treasure.

27

Ginny

Miss Bea enters the front room with a flurry of movement. "Oh, dear."

"What is it?" I set aside the book that I'm reading.

"I just returned from the mercantile, and Cora Whitley was there. In no uncertain terms she said she'd kill Mister Harold if she saw him anywhere near her property." Miss Bea paces the room. "With her pistol. Can you imagine?"

I inch to the edge of the sofa. "What do you mean? Whatever for?"

How could one murder a harmless cat? I've known old Missus Whitley was an ornery woman, but kill a pet?

Miss Bea sits sideways on the edge of her chair gripping one armrest with both hands. "She accused Mister Harold of *prowling* around attempting to mate with her *Sylvia*." Miss Bea mimics Missus Whitley's high and mighty tone.

I jump to my feet. "What shall we do?"

"I don't know." She turns her eyes to the ceiling as though in thought. "We can't keep him locked up."

She's right, we can't keep him locked up. Oh, that damn old woman. How dare she threaten the life of an innocent creature.

I'm pacing now. "Perhaps she should keep her precious *Sylvia* locked up," I grumble, indignantly.

Miss Bea turns to me and lets out a hearty laugh, one I've never heard from her before. A laugh I wouldn't believe if I weren't here to witness it myself. Whatever could be so funny about this? My brows furrow at her.

"Oh dear." Using her handkerchief, she wipes her tears of laughter from her eyes. "I was so mad at that woman I harrumphed and left the store without buying a single item."

She leans forward, still wiping her face. "Ginny, I wanted to *slap* her," she whispers the words while glancing around as if concerned someone else might hear.

"I don't blame you," I murmur back.

"I know how much you love Mister Harold, Ginny, but I'm afraid the only way to save his life is to send him to the ranch. Another mouser shall never hurt."

"But what about a mouser here?"

"We'll have to get a female that won't *mate with Sylvia*." She snorts and falls back into her chair.

As he does every night, Mister Harold slept beside me. I cried myself to sleep thinking about losing yet another love. I know he'll be fine at the ranch, just as Buck is. But like Buck, I won't get to see him every day and I'll miss him so.

I told Miss Bea I'd take Mister Harold out to the ranch this morning before going to work at Lenny's shop. But first, I set to making breakfast as I do every morning while Miss Bea has her devotions, a time of prayer and Bible reading in her room.

Mister Harold scratches at the front door.

"I do apologize, sir, but you'll have to wait to go outside. I must finish this meal first." *Poor soul.* I kiss him and head back to the kitchen.

A few moments later, Doc enters and makes his way to the coffee pot. His eyes are bloodshot and heavy, worn from a long night spent tending to a patient.

"Did you forget to let that cat out this morning? That darned thing was clawing something fierce at the door."

"Miss Bea is afraid Missus Whitley will shoot him so I'm keeping him in until after breakfast, then I'm taking him to the ranch."

Doc halts mid pour of his cream. "Oh heavens, I plum forgot all about that."

I hum to myself as I turn pancakes and bacon on the griddle.

"Ginny, I let that blasted cat out."

I spin around. "You didn't?" Panic works up my stomach and reaches for my throat.

"I sure did." He rubs his weary head.

I throw the spatula on the counter, grab my coat that hangs by the door, and run.

My breath comes in short, quick gasps, as I repeatedly call the cat's name.

Fear grips my chest as I look behind and up every tree, and down every alley making my way closer to the Whitley's house.

"Mister Harold," I continue to shout as tears stream down my face. If anything happens to that cat, my heart shall be shattered into a million pieces. *I'm so sorry.*

"Ginny?" Silas's voice calls from behind me. "What's happened?"

I rub my face with my hands and flail my arms as I recount Missus Whitley's threats against poor Mister Harold and how Doc accidentally let him out and now I can't find him.

Silas smiles, reaches in his pocket, and pulls out a handkerchief. "Here. Dry your face. I have time before I need to be on the job. I'll help you search for him."

When we near the Whitley's home, we hear the cries of a cat. I look to Silas in a panic and run. By the time I reach the side yard, the crying has ceased, but right up against the fence, in the light of day, Mister Harold is mounting Sylvia. I gasp and move to grab him, but Silas catches me.

"I don't believe interfering is the best idea." I can tell he's stifling a laugh.

I catch my breath. "That old woman will kill him if she sees him mating with her beloved feline." I feel the rise of bile at the back of my throat. "And how can you think this is humorous?"

Silas rubs his palm over his mouth to hide a grin. "They only need but a moment of pleasure. Can you truly deny them that?" He states this while still attempting to keep a smile at bay.

I wag my head and let out something that's part huff and

part laugh. He's right. "So, what do we do? Stand here and watch and wait till they're done? Give them privacy?"

He chuckles. "He won't need long."

Although I roll my eyes at this man's comment, what I truly wish to do is kiss his face. *Stop it, Ginny.*

I notice movement out of the corner of my eye and see that Mister Harold and Sylvia have parted ways, but they appear as if they could both go at it again.

"We'd better hurry and scoop him up," Silas replies.

"Yes, I need to get him to the ranch to keep him safe from that old lady." I nod towards the woman's house. "And then I need to find a female mouser to replace him."

"Oh, that's easy," Silas quips, grabbing Mister Harold by the nape of his neck as though he's repulsed by him.

I take the cat in my arms, hug and kiss him, so grateful he's still alive. "Mister Harold, that was a very naughty boy. You know you weren't to run off." When I raise my head, Silas is staring down at me with an amused grin. "What?"

"You truly love that mangy cat."

I cover Mister Harold's ears and whisper, "He is not mangy. He is beautiful."

Silas shrugs. "Well, I can get you a female cat. Calvin gave me Naomi."

"Naomi?"

"I named her after my mother." He gives a sheepish grin while rubbing the back of his neck.

My heart squeezes a little more. "That is the sweetest thing I've ever heard." Now I wish to hug him…and kiss him.

We flinch at Missus Whitley's voice. "Good morning, Reverend." She waves and smiles.

I wrap my coat around Mister Harold.

"Good morning, Missus Whitley." Silas waves back then puts his arm around my waist, guiding me in the opposite direction. "We better get out of here."

As I ride out to the ranch with Mister Harold curled up in my lap, I can't help but think of how Silas keeps turning up, how being around him feels so natural, and aching a little inside knowing we can never be.

28

Ginny

Light from the rising sun is making its way through the window, drowning out the light of the lamp from the table. I take a sip of my coffee and spread Rebecca's blackberry jam on a biscuit when there's a knock at the front door. Since Doc is the only physician in town, you never know what time of day or night someone shall need his assistance. I've learned that in my short time here.

I hear Doc's voice along with a man and woman. It doesn't concern me, so I enjoy my little breakfast before leaving for work.

Miss Bea's tone is high pitched and frantic, but I can't make out her words. She swishes down the hall and into the kitchen like a tornado.

"Oh, Ginny dear. Poor Roberta McCalister broke her foot this morning. Would you be able to clean the parsonage for her and do your washing later?"

"Of course. When does she need me to go?"

"She says she's there by eight o'clock sharp." Miss Bea lowers her voice to a whisper. "But I do believe as long as it gets done that's all that matters."

I smile in understanding. "When I finish eating, I'll let Lenny know I'll be in this afternoon. Is Missus McCalister well enough for me to get directions from her on how and what she needs me to do?"

"Oh yes, certainly." Miss Bea shakes her head and whirls back out of the room.

I can't help but wonder if Silas will be there. Perhaps I'm hoping to see him, if only a glimpse. But I also prefer he's not there lest he silently scrutinize the way I clean.

Once at the parsonage, a part of me is sad not to see the man, yet another part of me breathes a sigh of relief. It feels as though I'm intruding upon his space, and it would be uncomfortable if he were here.

It's a warm, sunny morning, so when I've finished dusting and scrubbing, I open windows to air the place out. After beating the rugs on the line, I put them back in place, and glance about, admiring what a fine job I've done. Deciding to pick flowers, I go in search of a vase or jar to put them in.

As I open the kitchen cabinet, I'm surprised to see Silas enter the room.

"Oh, I..." I don't know what to say. I feel like I've been caught doing something I shouldn't. "I was just looking for a vase. I thought I'd put some fresh flowers on the table for you."

His face lights up with pure joy, and I can see he's both

surprised and happy to see me. My breath hitches at his smile. He glances around with furrowed brows. "Where's Missus McCalister?"

"Oh, you didn't hear? She broke her foot early this morning and asked that I come clean the parsonage." I wipe my sweaty hands in my apron. "I'm finished, so I'll be going." I swing my braid over my shoulder and start for the door.

"Please, I just came home to make myself some dinner. Won't you join me?"

My jaw works up and down, but no words form. I'm sure the church folk would believe it's inappropriate of me to have a meal with the preacher, alone. And I should be leaving for Lenny's to get my washing done. Yet, I can't help but wish for time with this man.

He removes a loaf of bread from the box that sits on the counter. "Missus McCalister does a fine job of supplying me with fresh baked goods, and I have leftover roast beef from supper yesterday."

"All right then." I grab for the bread to start the meal, but he stops me.

"Oh no. You're my guest. Please." He gestures to the table. "Have a seat."

I've never had a man make me anything before. Well, except for the fellas, I suppose. But even if I were sick, I still prepared food for Jake. I don't know what he would have done had it been me who died first.

"Jam?" he asks, holding the jar out to me.

I stare down at my sandwich. *Who puts jam on their roast*

beef? "Uhhh."

"Don't tell me you've never had jam on roast beef," he remarks, spreading the thick, glossy fruit over his bread.

"Why would I?" I chuckle.

His brows shoot up. "Because it's incredible, that's why."

I shrug. "I suppose I could try a little."

With the knife, I place a small amount of the preserve on the corner of my sandwich and take a bite. I'm surprised to discover a sweet and savory flavor like no other, and I must admit, "This is quite excellent." Pulling the bread from the meat, I cover it in a thin layer of sweetness.

"I told you." He takes another chomp of his meal.

The conversation over lunch comes easily.

"Tell me," he says, nibbling on a slice of cheese. "Where are you from? Are your parents still living? I want to learn everything about you."

"Well let's see." I cross one leg over the other and sit back to get comfortable.

"My upbringing was one of privilege. Something I don't delight in. My father is an investor, often absent from home, no doubt due to his inability to endure my mother's company. He's a sharp businessman, but weak with his wife. She is both the captain and first mate of her home, and she runs a terribly tight ship. They have servants for every task—cooking, cleaning, running errands, dressing, even bathing. I loathed it. My parents host lavish gatherings, at which the governor, the chief of police, and the editor-in-chief of various newspapers and magazines are in attendance."

Silas tilts his head with a grin. "That sounds like a wonderful life to me."

I lean in. "It's not. My mother examined every garment I wore, every companion I had, and every action I took. My days were mostly spent devoted to my studies and reciting scripture."

I sip the warm creamy milk from the tin cup.

"I've come to learn that true wealth is not measured in coins, fine homes, or jewelry and costly china. It's not found in the latest fashions or in the ability to import luxuries from Paris. True wealth lies in having a roof over your head, food on your plate, health in your body, and love to warm your heart."

"I believe this is why Livvie, Lenny, and I share such a bond. We've experienced so much sorrow in our youth, and we'd never dare pass judgment upon one another for the choices we've made because of that suffering. We're three women who those we trusted most sought to break. Lucky for us, we just bent a little, but never broke."

"Here. Here." Silas raises his cup of milk.

I learn of his upbringing which, like Jake's, was much different than my own. We share humorous stories from our childhood, which brings a lot of laughter to the table. I find that tends to happen when I'm around him. I like the way I feel in his company, though I'm well aware that it's dangerous to feel this way, seeing that he's the preacher.

His arms rest upon the table and there's a twinkle in his eye as he leans towards me. "Well, I suppose I best be getting back to work before Matthews fires me."

I grab his plate, and he takes my arm, gentle but firm. "I'll clean this up." Our gazes meet and the familiar warmth of desire builds between us. His hand remains on my arm and his thumb brushes back and forth. I slowly rise from the chair, not breaking his hold. He stands gazing down at me with an intensity I haven't known in a long while. His eyes search my face, my mouth.

My lips part of their own accord, ready for his. But no, we mustn't do this.

"You best get back," I whisper. "I'll take care of this." I slide my arm from his hand and pull his plate from the table.

He clears his throat. "I suppose you're right." Taking his hat from the rack, he thanks me for the fine job I've done with the house. "Ginny?" he says, standing by the door. "Thank you for having dinner with me today. Believe it or not, it gets lonely over here."

I smile and dip my head. "Thank you for inviting me."

When he leaves, I realize my hands are shaking. I nearly kissed the preacher. I wish to kiss the preacher. No, I don't wish to *only* kiss him, I wish to wrap my bare body around him. I lean against the counter and give a noticeable sigh.

29

Silas

All I can think about is Ginny, sweet Ginny. How the day can change. I expected to go home for the noon meal and find that Missus McCalister had cleaned the place and gone. Never did I expect to find the beautiful blonde who's been running through my mind since she arrived in town.

As much as I wish for her to be mine, I know it can never work. She believes me to be an upstanding man of God. If only she knew the real me, what I've done, she wouldn't care to associate with me. I know taking her as my own is a fantasy that can never happen. Eventually the truth shall reveal itself and when it does, I don't want to lose her. But perhaps it is better to have loved and lost. Perhaps if she is mine, even for but a moment, it shall be more than if she had never been mine at all.

When I return home at the end of the workday, I discover fresh flowers on the table. She decided to leave them after all. I smile as I bend to take in their scent. When I move to my room to change, I see she's made the bed differently from Missus McCalister. I like it. She's turned down the quilt with the sheet, and she's propped two pillows nicely against the wall as there is no headboard. I smooth my hand over the turned down bedding imagining her touch against it.

If only I could find a way to see her outside of church.

Then I recall Missus McCalister's broken foot. This most likely means Ginny will be cleaning every week until the older woman heals. I sure hope so. Perhaps I'll have to forget my midday meal every Friday just so I can see her.

The McCalister supper table is always quiet. I insisted I could eat at home this evening, but the Missus wouldn't hear of it, stating the Simpson family brought more than enough food, considering she'll be down for a while and knowing that I join them for supper.

"Reverend Flynn," Missus McCalister breaks the mealtime silence. "I do apologize that I'm unable to clean the parsonage, but Ginny Price, she's such a lovely young lady. She said she is happy to take care of it until I'm healed."

So, Ginny will be back. My mouth is suddenly parched, and I fight to keep a straight face.

Missus McCalister goes on. "Did you notice she'd been there? How did she do?"

I'm sure mentioning that she and I had dinner together today would not be a good idea. Nor that I almost stole a kiss. No. I'll keep those facts to myself.

"Yes, she did a fine job. I'm very pleased." I quickly reach for my glass of milk.

Normally I'd argue that I can clean the house myself, but not this time. I don't want to do anything to dissuade Missus McCalister from sending Ginny over.

Grateful for the return of silence the remainder of the meal, I eat thinking of nothing but that golden haired woman who's doing things to me I'm quite sure I've never known.

30

Silas

Trudging through the snow from the church back to the parsonage, I'm pondering a leisurely day. We haven't worked since Wednesday due to the weather, so I'll most likely read and nap. Although it's Friday, I don't anticipate seeing Ginny this morning due to the storm we had overnight. It's a shame, because I do long to see her face.

As I near the back door, faint notes from the piano inside greet my ears. Perhaps she decided to come over after all. But why would she be playing the piano? Strange. Also, I can clean the house myself, it's not that serious of a matter. However, Missus McCalister is a rather serious woman when it comes to getting something done, and Ginny most likely fears this.

Not wishing to disturb her, I quietly remove my snowy boots and pour myself a cup of coffee, which I made before going out to shovel. I believe I should let her know I'm here and that I'll be in my room, so she needn't worry about cleaning it today. When I step into the sitting room, I come to a halt at the sight before me.

Ginny's playing the piano beautifully, and she has Naomi in her lap. I chuckle to myself remembering her holding and kissing that mangy cat, Mister Harold.

Her fingers go still over the keys. "What do you think of that, Naomi? Do you like that melody?" she asks the feline while snuggling Naomi in her neck and face.

"I thought it was quite beautiful." I take a sip of my coffee and lean against the doorframe.

The cat jumps from her lap, and she turns clutching her chest. "I didn't know you were there. I apologize." She begins to rise but I hold out my hand signaling for her to stay there.

"Please, stay where you are." I go to her, sitting the coffee cup on a crocheted doily atop the piano. Placing my fingers over the keys, I begin to play softly. "Where'd you learn to play?" I ask, delicately hitting each note while keeping my eyes on her.

She smiles. "Where'd *you* learn to play?"

"Ah, I asked first."

"My mother insisted upon it. I had to play for my parents' friends when they had parties. Sometimes I played at church." She joins in from her side of the piano and I remove one hand allowing her to be my other.

I watch her fingers move over the keys. "My mother insisted upon it as well," I state. "But we were poor and had no parties. Our piano was old and out of tune."

Our closeness heats me—her shoulder against mine. Her left hand rests in her lap, and I find myself wanting to take my right hand, resting upon my knee, and gently hold hers. We continue to play as if we were one—softly, delicately. The heat that's been building overtime is growing more intense between us in this moment.

She glances up at me then back to our hands. "Do you know 'Buffalo Gals'?" she asks. With a smile, she bites her bottom lip, lifts her left hand, and jovially pounds out the song.

I must raise my voice above the music. "As a matter of fact, I do." I bring my right hand to the board and begin to play along with her.

She reaches over my right hand and plays to my left, so I reach over her left hand to play to her right. We're banging on the keys making a mess of the poor song, but we're having a grand time, laughing uncontrollably. I'm certain Ginny has lifted herself from the bench several times to reach over me.

I belt out the lyrics, off key I might add.

She was the prettiest gal I've ever seen in my life
In my life, in my life
And I wished to the Lord she'd be my wife
Then we would part no more

Then Ginny bellows out the next lines.

Oh, yes, dear boy, I'm coming out tonight
Coming out tonight, coming out tonight
Oh, yes, dear boy, I'm coming out tonight
And we'll dance by the light of the moon

Finally, we stop with a banging grand finale. She's leaning against me laughing with her hands to her belly. When she peers up at me our laughter dies down, our breaths are heavy. I glance at her lips, soft and subtle, then to her eyes that move to my lips.

"May I kiss you?" I whisper.

She moves closer with a nod. "Yes."

The scent of lavender on her stirs my senses as I tenderly claim her lips with mine. Pulling back, I study her face for any sign that I should stop. Her eyes flutter open, and I gently cradle her chin and draw her in for another delicate kiss. My tongue traces the soft fullness of her lips, and she parts them for me. I slide in and make an exploration of her warm, wet mouth.

I have a renewed sense of freedom as our kiss deepens and our breaths become more shallow. She places her hand upon my leg, and I grow hard at her touch. Taking her hand in mine, our tongues entwine more passionately.

I find myself longing for more of her, but I know the consequences could be disastrous, so I resolve to restrain myself before this goes further. I pull away and rest my head against hers. She leans in for another kiss, her hand resting gently upon my chest. Then, drawing away slightly, her eyes search mine.

"Oh my," she whispers. "What are we doing?"

I shake my head and grin. "I'm certain you just kissed me." I trust she can detect the amusement in my tone.

"Perhaps I should go." But she moves in for another kiss, her breaths heavy.

She doesn't wish to leave, and I don't want her to. "It's probably best." I reclaim her mouth again, hard and deep, wanting nothing more than to lift her up and carry her to my bed.

Once more, our lips part ways. "I'll think of a reason to give

Missus McCalister as to why I didn't finish cleaning today."

I nod, unable to take my eyes off her beautiful face. The urge to touch her breasts grows strong.

She nibbles her bottom lip, eyeing my mouth hungrily. "I best be going."

The clock on the wall tick tocks, tick tocks.

I lean in to share another kiss, taking her face in my hand before my fingers make their way over her cheek and down her neck.

She captures my hand before it can move any further. "We shouldn't be doing this."

I'm certain she believes this is unbecoming of a preacher. I suppose she's correct, even if it does feel completely natural. "I understand." I pull away and move a couple of inches down the bench to make space between us. "I apologize."

She glides her fingers over the piano keys as if feeling them for the first time. "I can't believe I kissed the reverend."

I clutch my chest and lean away exaggeratedly as if I've been shot.

She giggles.

Should I feel remorseful? I don't. I long to kiss her repeatedly. I long to take her in my arms and hold her, bury my face in her blonde locks, inhaling her lavender scent.

"Trust me, Silas, I'm not the one for you."

"How do you know what's for me?"

She wrings her hands and glances around before peering back at me. "I'm just not."

The clock continues to tick.

She gestures with great animation, her eyes appearing to

hold nothing and everything at once. "I'm just saying, I'm not the one for you." She stops and looks at me. "Oh, I'm so sorry that I've caused you to sin." She rises from the bench, and I take her arm.

"It's all right," I state, providing her with a smile of reassurance. "We have free will. You can't cause me to do anything I don't wish."

Her smile portrays a combination of relief and sadness.

"I tell you what," I add, taking my coffee cup from the piano. "Why don't I go to the church, and you can clean so you don't get in trouble with Missus McCalister, *and* you don't feel like you must be dishonest on account of me. How does that sound?"

"Oh, I can't push you out into the cold."

"It's fine. I need to prepare for Wednesday Bible study anyway, and what better place to do that than in the church? I already have the woodstove burning over there anyhow."

She peers at me with those wintery blue eyes. "Thank you, Silas."

Upon my return to the parsonage, I notice the house has a fresh scent, and the kitchen is tidied. Ginny's placed an extra rug by the backdoor for my boots. When I go to my room, I see she's made my bed, once again with the quilt and sheet turned down together, not a wrinkle in it. The pillows are fluffed, propped against the wall, and my heart swells at the thought of the care she's given to every detail. Laying back on my bed I can't help but feel aroused by this. "Oh, Ginny. I'd give anything for another kiss from you." I sigh into the room, closing my eyes with the remembrance of our earlier encounter.

31

Ginny

It's Friday, which means I'm cleaning the parsonage. This has been the longest week of my life, and all I've been able to think of is Silas's mouth on mine. I sigh as I stroll along the street towards the church.

After Sunday and Wednesday services, he gave my hand a gentle squeeze as if to share a message only I could interpret. How I long to bury my face in the smoothness of his neck and take in his intoxicating scent of warm spices and citrus. I close my eyes, inhaling deeply through my nose as if his fragrance lingers before me.

Although I'm fearful everyone can see what's happening between us, I must admit I look forward to attending church for the first time in my life, not for the message, but for the man behind it. The man whose dark hair I dream of running my fingers through. The man whose smooth-shaven cheek I imagine resting my hand on. The man who certainly knows how to embrace a woman. Unlike with Joe, Silas's mouth on mine felt natural and familiar.

I've yearned for him since we sealed our longing with a kiss. A part of me hopes beyond hope that he arrives home for dinner before I leave today. I must see him. I have to know if this is all real or if I imagined it.

Closing my eyes, I take in all that Mother Nature has to offer me—the scent of damp earth, the feel of a gentle breeze, and the sound of a crow cawing in the distance. What a beautiful morning it is. I can't recall the last time I felt so lighthearted. I yearn to sing along with the little birds who greet the day.

Entering the house through the kitchen, I remove my shoes and step into the sitting room in search of Naomi.

"Ginny." Silas, I realize, is pacing.

"Is everything all right?"

He moves towards me pushing his hands through his hair. "I was hoping to see you before I left this morning."

He swipes his hands down his breeches.

"What is it?" I ask, worry setting in.

Someone must have learned what we did.

He gently presses me against the wall, widening his stance as he lowers himself to my level. "You are all I've been able to think about." His eyes are upon my lips.

A flame burns within me as I peer back at his. As much as I want this, I know it can never be. I, we, are setting ourselves up for heartache. My mind is conflicted.

"Silas, we can't do this, as much as we may want to."

His stare is intense. His breath heavy. "I've never longed for anything more."

"I can't be a preacher's wife."

He slowly wags his head staring deeply into my eyes as if they have him in a trans. "You don't have to be."

"It's taken me a long time to get to this point since Jake…" I glance away. "I can't give my heart to someone only to be hurt."

"I won't hurt you." He trails his thumb over my cheek, his eyes willing me to give into him. There's a sense of truth in his words. In his face. How I can say no to this man, I don't have a clue. I too feel as though I've never wanted anything more.

Something comes over me, and I take hold of his shirt and tug. "Are you just going to stand there staring at me, or are you going to kiss me?"

Knowing he has my full permission, he wraps one arm around my waist and the other braces against the wall behind me. His mouth meets mine and our warm tongues embrace in a sweet dance I don't ever want to end.

I wrap my arms around his neck and run my fingers up through the back of his hair.

"I've missed you," he breathes, trailing his knuckles down my face.

"I've missed you too. I was beginning to believe last week was a dream."

He takes my chin, lifting it, then lays a soft kiss on the corner of my mouth. "Me too," he sighs. "I have to go, but I'll come back for lunch, if you'll wait for me."

I lean in to share another peck of his lips and he pulls me

hard against his body, presses his mouth to my head, and then to my lips once more. "I'll expect more of this when I return."

I nod not wanting to let go of him. This beautiful man has my head spinning. I'm almost afraid if I step away from him, I'll succumb to a fainting spell. Or worse, that I'll wake up and realize it's all been a dream.

I make a point of having the noon meal ready for when he returns. Looking down at the table, I'm pleased with myself and hope he's impressed with the fact that I can do more than clean.

My head jerks up at the sound of the door swinging open. Silas tosses his hat to the floor and shuts the door with his foot in one fell swoop. He rushes to me and kisses me like a man who's just returned from war. I wrap my arms around him reciprocating his affection. "I was so worried you'd change your mind," he breathes between laps of our tongues.

His gaze falls to the table, and he smiles, still holding me. "You made dinner."

"I hope you enjoy it."

"I'm certain it's as good as it looks."

My heart skips a beat at the joy on his face.

The meal is filled with more stories from our lives, and I love how easy our conversations are. *It's like we were made for each other.* This thought stops me. It's like we were made for each other. But Silas is a preacher. And I? I'm not a Christian.

I force a smile to halt the tears that fight to come.

When I reach for Silas's plate to clear the table, he moves his chair out and pulls me onto his lap. "What's the matter?" He runs his thumb over my cheek, and I shake my head afraid to speak. "Was it something I said?"

How can I be upset with this man? He's caring and gentle and kind and funny and fun and…"What are we doing?" I must know what's happening between us.

He buries his face into the sleeve of my blouse and closes his eyes.

"What are we doing?" I repeat, taking his chin, forcing him to look up at me.

"I don't know, Ginny. All I know is you're all I think about, since the day I laid eyes on you at Doc's when I officiated Justus and Livvie's wedding. I've been able to think of little else. And last week when we finally kissed?" He lets out a groan, almost a growl. Pulling my face to him, he pecks my lips. "We'll figure it out. I promise we'll figure it out."

As I walk to Lenny's to tend to the days' washing, I hear Jake's voice. He's been coming to me less frequently, which concerns me. Am I forgetting about him? No. I'll never forget him. Perhaps he's forgetting me.

It's time for you to move on.

"I can't. It's not right."

It is right, Ginny. Silas is a good man.

I know I have Jake's blessing, but I'm so torn.

I can't fight the tears any longer. I wish I were alone to scream and fight against Jake's words that I regard with my heart. "I don't want your blessing, Jake. I want you. There was no wondering if we were right for one another or wondering how we'd be together." I'm fearful of the future.

That's not true, Ginny. You came from a wealthy family who didn't want you with a poor man's son. There's more to Silas than you know. But you must trust him.

Jake's words sting. He's correct. My mother fought to keep us apart.

Jake and I did not attend the same school because I had the best private tutors New York had to offer, while he attended a small schoolhouse where the common folk, as my parents would say, went. We met through acquaintances and became fast friends. I loved him from the beginning.

When I reached my teen years, my mother feared Jake and I were becoming too close, so she forbade me to have anything to do with him. She and I got into many shouting matches over him. One time she locked me in my room. Only she, no one else, was to bring me food and fetch my chamber pot. When my father discovered what she'd done, he demanded I be freed immediately. I believe that's the only time he'd ever put his foot down with her. I had never seen him so angry.

I'm only met with silence when I ask Jake what his words mean to me and Silas.

When I enter Lenny's, I'm so relieved to find that we're alone that I break down in tears.

"Oh mercy, let me get you a drink," she announces, leaving

the room.

I drop onto the sofa, bury my face in my hands, and sob.

"What happened?" she asks, handing me a glass of bourbon.

I take a sip, letting the warm heat trickle down my throat.

She produces a handkerchief, and I wipe my nose. "I'm so confused, Lenny. And I believe I may be attempting to replace my husband."

"Sugar, your husband's been gone for years. Don't you think it's more than time to move on without the worry of replacing him?"

"I didn't ask for him to die, Len."

"Of course you didn't, but such is life." She slaps her hands in her lap. "Now, tell me what on earth is going on."

I take another swallow of the whiskey. "It's Silas Flynn."

I'm expecting to see surprise upon her face, but none shows there. "Go on."

"He's a preacher, Lenny. And I don't wish to replace Jake."

Lenny takes the glass from my hand and downs the last of the drink. "You deserve to be loved, Ginny, even by a preacher." She stares at me as if she's daring me to contradict her words. "Now…" She straightens as if ready to take this head on. "Did you lie with him?"

The surprise must show upon my face now. "No. No, I didn't lie with him. We kissed."

Her mouth turns up into a smile.

"I can't live that life, Lenny. The life of a preacher's wife. I can't be someone I'm not."

She pats my knee with a sigh. "No, that you can't do."

32

Ginny

Because it's Friday, I have no choice but to let myself into the parsonage to clean. And, like the other cleaning days, I find myself in Silas's home amongst his belongings. This time I hope to be in and out without seeing him.

I saw him again at the Sunday morning service and Wednesday evening service. Both times I did my best to avoid him or avoid making eye contact with him. During the services, I mostly gazed aimlessly into the Bible in my lap to keep from watching him and thinking about what we did, or what I wish to do with him.

While washing the tin coffee mug he drank from this morning, I can't help but think of his lips on it. Changing the sheets of his bed, I imagine him lying there with his shirt off. I take his pillow and inhale his spicy fragrance.

"Ginny?"

Silas.

I yelp and throw the pillow on the bed. "You startled me. I'm sorry, I was just changing your linens." I grab at the bedding to remove it. So lost in my thoughts of him I didn't even hear him enter the house. Surely I'm as pink as a piglet.

"You know you can't avoid me forever."

I glance up to see him leaning against the doorway of his bedroom. A smile plays upon his lips.

"I don't know what you mean." I shake a clean cotton sheet over the bed.

"I believe we should just be honest that we can't stop thinking about each other."

I peer at him and his expression tugs at my heart. *This is going to hurt.*

With a sense of defeat, I toss the quilt in my hands onto the bed, then step toward him. "You are a preacher, and I…." I point my finger between the two of us. "*We* can't be, *ever*. I can never be a preacher's wife." My voice is stern. Not accusatory, just stating the truth.

He reaches out, draws me into him, and kisses my mouth so softly I almost don't feel it. But I do, to my core, where a fire sparks. I give in and wrap my arms around him as lust bubbles within me. He lifts my body and carries me to his bed where our mouths are hungry, and our hands roam free over our clothing. I welcome his earthy, sweet scent and allow it to wash over me— down my chest, my legs, and into my toes.

A hard knock at the kitchen door jolts us apart. Mister McCalister stands on the back porch. I gasp and Silas runs his fingers through his hair, eyes darting about. The heat of guilt rushes up my body and into my face. Instinct causes me to seek refuge behind the bedroom door. I work to hold my breath steady rather than closing it off completely.

"Mister McCalister, I wasn't expecting to see you this morning." Silas's voice shakes slightly as he attempts to sound cheery.

There's a moment of silence.

I take a slow inhale and exhale as I close my eyes while pressing myself harder against the wall.

"The Missus asked that I bring these biscuits to you."

"Oh, please convey my thanks to her. I always appreciate her baking."

I hear nothing but the blood pulsing in my ears. *What is going on out there?*

"I was expecting to find Ginny here, not you. You don't have work today?"

"Yes, I woke up late then thought I'd go ahead and wash up my dishes here before Ginny arrives. I don't feel right about her having to clean up after me."

Silas just lied to Mister McCalister. Oh dear, I am turning him into someone he's not. I clench my eyes feeling a guilt like no other.

"I see."

A bird hops from branch to branch on the pine tree outside the window.

"Yes, well please thank Missus McCalister. But I had better head out before Mister Matthews thinks I've up and quit." Silas makes another attempt to sound upbeat, but there's a nervousness that plays at the edge of his words.

"All right then."

There's a clomp of boots before the door creaks closed.

A wave of relief sweeps over me, and I feel like I can truly breathe as I lean my head against the wall. I can't live like this. In time, Silas will resent me if we continue. Our beliefs are too opposite for us to authentically come together.

I begin to finish making up the bed when Silas comes in and brings me into his arms. "That was close. I believe he was suspicious. When he was eyeing the clean dishes on the cloth beside the wash bin, I told him I had washed them." He peppers kisses over my cheek and down my neck.

I stand motionless, tears spilling over.

He recoils, examining my face. "It's all right." He gently wipes a tear away with his thumb.

"I can't do this."

He takes a step back, still holding onto my waist. "What are you saying?"

"I'm sorry, but this is over." I sniffle and wipe my nose with the back of my hand. Being ladylike is of no importance to me in this moment.

"Please, don't."

I can't look at his face knowing I will only see a pleading in his eyes.

"I have to finish my job here today. I need time to think, and cleaning will help me do that." I glance around to avoid looking at him.

He lets go of me and takes another step back. "Ginny, please."

I hear the beseeching in his voice and see it in this stance.

I busy myself with the quilt again. My mind is as full and jumbled as that one drawer in Miss Bea's kitchen that has no purpose but to collect odds and ends.

"Silas, you don't understand."

He takes two quick strides and spins me to face him. "No, *you* don't understand." His eyes pleading. "But I need you to trust me. It'll take some time, but we can be together. I just ask that you're patient with me." He leans in laying his lips on mine, soft and tender.

The urge to give into him once more is so strong I hold my breath and squeeze my eyes.

He steps away and I shift my gaze down. The pain in my heart is like the blue of a flame.

"No," I say. "You're the one who doesn't understand. *We* can never be." My gaze falls on the chest of drawers just beyond him where a wash basin sits beside his bottle of Bay Rum aftershave. "I'm going to ask that Missus McCalister find someone else to clean the parsonage from now on."

I dare to look up at him this time. My chest squeezes at the sadness in his eyes. He shoves his hands into the pockets of his trousers. I look away as he continues to stare at me, as if he's trying to find something he's missing. Something that shall save us. Then he nods his head and turns.

The kitchen door creaks open and closed. I collapse onto his bed, releasing all the emotions that I've locked up inside.

33

Ginny

My stomach flutters as the wagon comes to a halt in Sutton's Creek. It feels wonderful to be back. Spring is in the air, and the mountain town is buzzing with activity. It appears the sunshine and warmer temperatures have everyone out of their homes and into the streets.

The gentleman who's given me a ride up the mountain is kind enough to offer his hand in helping me down from the wagon.

"The melting snow has made everything a mess. Watch your step."

My boots squish into the muddy road as I descend the carriage.

I recall all too well how mucky the soil can get this time of year. "I'm accustomed to it, but thank you."

My bag is clutched in my hands as I take a step and close my eyes inhaling the sweet mountain air. Home. There's a tingling of excitement that makes its way up my spine.

I left Laurel Springs on such short notice I didn't have time to write Mirna and alert her to my visit. It's my hope she'll have a room available.

The anticipation builds as I open the door of my friend's hotel and hear the familiar ring of bells that hang just above me.

"Hello, Mirna?" The earthy scent of sage greets me and brings joy to my heart. I recall the first day I set foot here and found the odor to be overwhelming. Now I welcome it. It's soothing and relaxes my mind.

"Can I help you?" A girl with long dark braids moves through the beaded doorway. She could have been Mirna in another life, only taller.

"I'm Ginny Price. Is Mirna in?"

I've never known Mirna to not be here.

The girl's eyes show sorrow as she folds her hands together and gracefully places them upon the counter.

"My grandmother has told me much about you. You were good friends."

Were?

"I'm afraid she passed a couple of weeks ago."

I reach for the counter as my head feels light.

The girl rushes around the wooden barrier. "Please, come sit." She helps me to a chair in the corner. "I wrote to you, but I suppose there wasn't time for you to receive the news."

The remembrance of hearing Mirna's voice comes to me. *Had she already passed?*

How is it possible that my friend is no longer here? Then I remember how she'd speak of those who've died are just on the other side of the veil, and I feel her arm upon my shoulder. My eyes dart, expecting to see her standing there, but it's only air.

The girl chuckles. "You see her?"

I notice the young woman's eyes twinkling as she smiles down on me.

"No, but I feel her." Will she think me mad?

"Yes. She is here."

"Are you…Can you…?" I don't know how to ask if she has the gift like her grandmother. Mirna said it ran in the family but had never mentioned it beyond herself.

"Yes, I have my grandmother's gift. So does my father." She pats my hand. "Come. There's something she wished for you to have."

I follow her into what used to be Mirna's living quarters. She motions for me to sit at the table while she places her grandmother's teacup and saucer in front of me.

"She wants you to have her tea set. She said you two had many laughs and cries over tea and cookies. But first, we must drink to her." She smiles as she pours the pine needle tea into my cup. Her skin is darker than Mirna's, and I wonder if her mother is full blood. Mirna had told me her own mother was of Mexican descent, but her father was a white man.

"Do you live around here?" I watch the girl's gentle movements, and I feel at peace in her presence.

"I live here, for now. Father believes we need to sell, but I know this business meant a lot to my grandmother and I'd like to keep it going for her." She chuckles, holding her cup with both hands. "Father doesn't believe I'm safe here, but I told him if Grandmother could remain safe, so can I."

He's probably concerned for her safety because she's young and beautiful. And he knows the white man cannot be trusted.

"I have my gun and I'm an expert shot. Father made sure of that."

"I'm sorry, I didn't get your name."

"Everyone calls me Rosy."

"That's beautiful, and it suits you."

"Thank you." Rosy's cup clinks against the saucer.

"I'm sorry to learn about your grandmother, she was a dear friend."

"Sorry for us, but wonderful for her. She's free now."

I study the flower pattern on the tea pot. Pinks, greens, yellows. "Yes, I suppose you're right. I wish I had been here."

"She passed peacefully. She said to me, 'I rest now, Rosy.' And then she closed her eyes and let out a long breath."

"Was she ill?"

"She knew it was her time. She sent word to my father, so we came and sat with her until her spirit left her body." Rosy pats my hand. "It was a beautiful day."

This young woman is wise beyond her years.

"I'm sure it was." I can't help but smile back at her glowing face.

After some time of getting to know one another and discussing her grandmother, Rosy hands me a key to one of the rooms. "No charge for you," she states when I dig in my bag for my pocketbook.

I welcome the cool air with notes of the earthy, piney scent of juniper that greets me as I make my way to the new restaurant a block away from Mirna's hotel. I intend to go over the ridge to visit the fellas today. Although I don't have Buck, I do carry a revolver.

"What can I get for you?" A rather large woman stands before me, blocking my view of the window that looks out upon an aspen grove.

"Coffee, please."

"Would you like to eat? You look like you could use some food." Her eyes rove over me.

My smile falters. "Yes, food would be wonderful." I had better fill up. It's going to be a long day.

"Well, what would you like to eat?"

"Oh, I'm sorry." I shake my head, pressing my fingers to my temple. An attempt to summon a proper thought I suppose. "Eggs. Eggs would be lovely. And bacon and sourdough toast with butter." After the news of Mirna, I fear what I might find when I reach camp.

"Very well."

When the woman leaves, I notice a gentleman who resembles Silas sitting at a table that flanks the window, and my mind involuntarily goes to the man I left behind. I wonder if Silas reads the newspaper while eating his breakfast. Before I know it, the man near the window is smiling at me, and I realize I've been staring at him. I give a quick thin-lipped grin and turn away, heat rising in my cheeks. How terribly embarrassing.

The meal is lovely, although I spend the entire time deliberately forcing myself not to look at the man sitting at the window.

As I sift through my purse for the coins to pay for my meal, the thought of heading up to camp fills me with dread. I can't shake the uncertainty of what I might find once I get there. I'm also unsure of where to go from here with my life. If only Mirna were here to provide her sage wisdom.

Go back to Laurel Springs. Her whisper tickles my ear.

"Your meal's been paid for," says the woman as I hold out my hand with the change.

"Paid for?" I repeat, still holding out my hand.

"Yes, the gentleman sitting over there paid your bill." She points to the man I've been working to avoid. I smile sheepishly at him, and he raises his cup to me.

As I turn, I bump into a giggling girl, causing me to drop my coins to the floor. Although I'm certain neither of us is at fault, I apologize and bend down to collect my money.

"I beg your pardon; my wife can be a bit silly at times. Let me help you." The man bends down grabbing at my loot.

My hand stills at the voice. *Big Joe.* The girl is still giggling. Perhaps she's drunk. How sad to be drunk this time of day.

His beard is trimmed and his dark hair cut short. Gone are the curls.

"Joe."

It's him all right. He peers at me through dark lashes.

"You two know each other?" The girl has a southern accent.

He hands over my money without a word.

"Joe?" she questions. "What's going on? How do you know this woman?" She places a hand on her hip.

He's as bewildered as I am.

I straighten and hold my hand out to the girl who can't

be more than 17 or 18. "Virginia. Virginia Price. Joe worked with my husband years ago." I know it's best to appear as old acquaintances, for his sake.

"Oh, how nice." She places a large grin on her face and shakes my hand. "I'm Imogene, Joe's wife." She holds up her finger to show me a plain gold band. "We just wed yesterday at the courthouse, didn't we sweetheart?"

Joe looks to be in shock as he stares at me. I can sense his longing for me, and it fills me with sorrow, especially after all this time. The girl runs her palm over a small but protruding belly then leans in to whisper to me. "We weren't plannin' on marryin', but…" She giggles and splays all ten fingers out wide. "Oops."

I glance between them both, uneasy. "Congratulations." I give a shaky smile. "Well, I best be going. I'm heading up to camp, and that's going to be quite the day. It was lovely meeting you, Imogene." I turn to the man standing quietly beside her. "Joe."

I walk briskly down the sidewalk, working to make sense of what I just witnessed when there is a pull of my arm.

"Joe."

"Ginny." Pain shows upon his face.

I turn and face him full on. Confused as to why I'm seeing him, or why he ran after me.

He shoves his hand through his hair in frustration. "I…"

I lay a hand upon his arm. "I wish you and your wife the best, Joe."

185

The melting snow makes the creek sound more like a river as the water rushes down the mountain and over rocks and boulders. I cup the frigid liquid in my palm and take a sip. Its coolness stings the back of my throat as I swallow.

It feels wonderful to traverse this path again.

Will this be my home once more? I can't help but wonder what the future holds for me.

I wipe my hands on my coat and march on to camp.

My cabin comes into sight and the urge to run is strong, but smoke curling from the chimney brings me to a halt. My heart squeezes in my chest as I place my hand to my mouth attempting to keep the tears at bay. But I fail and weep into my palm as my body shakes.

It's not my cabin. My cabin burned down. Someone has rebuilt in the exact same spot.

What did you expect?

I suppose I don't know what I expected.

I wipe away the tears, deciding I'll introduce myself.

It's strange to knock on your own door. Only, I must remind myself yet again that it's not my door.

"Ginny." Tucker's face shows joy at seeing me, and a relief washes over my body causing my eyes to brim with emotion.

"Oh, Ginny." He takes me in his arms and squeezes me tight. "Please, come in."

It's a simple one room home just as Jake and I had. Only, I eye another door.

"It leads out to a lean-to." Tucker opens it and I see wood stacked neatly inside.

He motions toward the table. "I took up your claim." He rubs the back of his neck. "I hope you don't mind."

I'm still peering around, taking it all in.

"I wouldn't want anyone else to have it," I say, and mean it.

He smiles that boyish grin. "I have rabbit stew on the back of the stove. Would you like some?"

"I'd love some."

When I'm finished eating, Tucker walks with me up to camp where he gives two loud whistles.

Old Man Marshall stumbles out of the outhouse shrugging into his suspenders. "Well I'll be damned."

I swallow past a lump in my throat at the sight of his red face. He's fighting back tears too.

"Boys, our Ginny's back," he hollers, wrapping me in a hug with tears streaming down his face.

Lee pokes his head out of a tent cradling a child in his arms. *That must be Fern's little one.*

Tucker had told me how Lee and Fern had taken a liking to one another when Lee took her to Sutton's Creek for the midwife. The fellas were surprised when they returned together, married, and set up a tent for themselves.

Marsh insisted on putting logs on the hot coals to get a fire going so we could visit like "old times."

Old times.

So much here is the same, but even more is different. It's not the home I once knew and loved. Although, I could set up my own tent and go back to washing for the fellas, and Fern and her baby boy.

Tucker offers me to stay in his cabin for the night while he sleeps in Marsh's tent with him.

And just like old times, we pass the bottle of whiskey and dance to Lee's fiddle. Then, Tucker walks me down to the cabin and sees to it that the fire's stoked and the lantern's lit.

The next morning, I wrap myself around the stones at Jake's gravesite.

"Oh, Jake." Emotions overtake my body as I cry into the crevices of the rocks. "I miss you."

After some time, an eagle swoops down, letting out a high-pitched whistle. I lift my chin and watch it in awe. It's a sign and I must heed its message.

This is no longer my home. I must spread my wings and fly.

34

Ginny

Silas stands at the pulpit with a shadow of whiskers covering his face. He peers out over the room and his eyes land on me. Our stares are intense, and my insides turn molten. He clears his throat and begins to speak, but there's a nervous quiver in his voice.

"Good evening, Church."

I wonder if his behavior has to do with me. Thankfully for me, Missus McCalister found someone else to clean the parsonage, and since I have been out of town, I haven't seen him in a couple of weeks.

It pains me to watch him. The first Sunday after I ended things between us, I pretended to be unwell. Of course, Miss Bea insisted Doc look me over, but he stated it was a woman's ailment and told me to rest and drink an herbal tea concoction he provided. After I became "well", I decided it was the perfect time to make a visit to see Mirna. Unfortunately, I was unable to spend time with my friend, but I had a lovely visit with Rosy, and even spent a few days in camp with the fellas. I was pleased to learn that Tucker took over my and Jake's claim.

After Silas stumbles through the blessing to begin, he opens his Bible. "Let us go to Esther chapter one, verse one. Now when King David…" He closes his eyes and hangs his head. "I'm sorry folks. When King Xerxes…" For the next hour, it's as if his body is here, but his mind is not, as he falters through the sermon.

As he stands at the back of the church wishing everyone a good night, I hear a remark about him being unwell and offerings of prayers. I stay back to speak with him after all is out the door. I have to know if he's truly ill.

"Silas?"

His eyes avoid me.

"Are you all right?" I dip my head to look into his face.

He peers at his calloused hands while rubbing them together. It's so quiet in the building that I can hear them moving against one another. "Like Missus Whitley said, I just need rest."

"Are you certain? Have you seen Doc?"

His eyes are rimmed red. "I'll be just fine."

Not knowing what else to say, I nod and head for the door.

"Ginny."

I turn towards his voice. His eyes glisten, his arms hang at his sides, and his shoulders sag. A broken man stands before me.

He holds out his hand. "I haven't been able to stop thinking about you and it's eating me up something terrible. When I learned you left town, I thought it was for good and feared I'd go mad. I don't know how Justus did it when Livvie left."

I close the door of the church then walk back and take his hand guiding him to a pew. "You're not alone in your thoughts."

"Oh, Ginny." He sighs a breath of relief and places his hand on my face, searching my eyes.

I shake my head. "But we're just not right for one another." I place my hand over his. "I can't be what you need me to be."

"I just need you to be you. That's all I ask. I wish for you to be just the way you are and never change."

He leans in and kisses me, and my body relaxes under his touch.

"I can't think straight without you. Please, I need you so badly." He lays a trail of soft kisses along my neck.

"You don't understand." I gently push him back, still afraid to confess that we don't share the same faith, but perhaps this is the time. He won't think so fondly of me once he hears the truth.

I take a deep breath. "Silas, I only come to these services because I live under the Peterson's roof, and I wish to respect their beliefs. However…" I fidget with the corner of the Bible sitting in my lap before looking him in the eyes. "Silas, I'm not a Christian. That's why we can't be together. Can't you see?"

Relief at my words appears to wash over him and tumble out into a laugh. "Oh, Ginny. It's all right. I promise you, it's all right." He takes my chin in his fingers and smiles brightly into my eyes. He runs his tongue along his bottom lip, leans in, and presses his lips to mine.

I open to receive his tongue, a touch that I've sorely missed. I place my hands on his whiskered face as he slowly moves from my mouth to my cheek and down to my neck.

An ache moves down the center of my body and I long to feel his caress in that most sensitive place. His lips return to mine and we kiss deeply, passionately.

"I need you, Ginny," he whispers into my mouth as his hand makes its way to my breast.

Even I don't feel comfortable being this intimate in the house of the Lord. It feels wrong to the people who believe it's a sacred place.

I take his hand and move it away. "We can't do this here."

His eyes search mine as if looking for answers.

"I'll go out the back door to the parsonage. You go out front then walk around to the road and come to the kitchen door."

I nod.

He smiles and places a tender kiss between my eyes.

"It would seem we've gotten ourselves into quite a predicament, haven't we?" he whispers against my lips.

Silas has me pressed against the kitchen door. The light of the moon fills the room. I crave this man in ways that I know would be more sinful than a kiss.

His lips return to mine, so tender, but I long for more. I know my thoughts aren't in proper order. But if he doesn't care, then I don't either. Laying my palm against his unshaven face, I explore the recesses of his mouth with my tongue. Heat continues to build between us, and I unbutton the collar of his shirt as he kisses along my jaw.

"We shouldn't be doing this," I whisper breathlessly.

"You're right." He brings his mouth back to mine and I open, happily letting him in to traverse my tongue once more. His hardness presses against my groin.

Could it be that he's been married in the past? He certainly knows what he's doing. A wife has never been mentioned, yet much of his life before Laurel Springs seems to be a mystery, aside from his childhood.

"Ginny, will you come to my bed with me?"

I grin mischievously. "I feared you'd never ask."

Once in the bedroom, he closes the door. "Take off your clothes," he commands, and I become a little wetter at his order.

As he lights the oil lamp, his eyes remain on me. Gently, he blows on the match, sending a curl of smoke that lingers in the air. A tingle spreads through my body as he undoes the buttons of his shirt, his gaze fixated on my every move. I watch his tongue run along his bottom lip and my breath hitches.

As his shirt slips to the floor, the muscles of his frame ripple with strength, then my fingers twitch at the sight of his erect girth.

He extends his hand to me. "Come here," he orders, his voice low.

I stand before him, only adorned with the stone that hangs from my neck, lamp light glistening off each edge. His eyes rove my body before he turns me to face the mirror that is placed in the corner of the room. "You're even more magnificent than I imagined."

Not being accustomed to seeing myself naked, I cast my gaze to the floor.

"Ahhh, there's no need to be bashful," he whispers against

my ear. "Your body is exquisite, and I want you to watch me enjoy it."

Goosebumps form over my skin as he trails kisses down my neck and onto my shoulder as his hardness strains against my backside. My knees weaken at his touch. This is an experience I've never known before, but I find it quite exciting.

He studies my reflection in the glass as he slowly glides his palms up my arm and over my breasts, delicately tracing the hardened peaks. His breath is warm against my face as his hand travels down my belly and between my legs, where a finger slips into my wet entrance. I inhale sharply.

"Oh, yes," he moans as together we watch his finger slide in and out.

I groan and close my eyes, laying my head back onto his shoulder. A shiver runs down my body as he continues to lay soft, wet kisses on my neck, and I reach behind to hold onto his hips for support.

"Mmm, that's it. Enjoy that."

My breaths are heavy as I move with the need of his fingers gliding through my slick center.

Compelled to watch him further, I open my eyes and raise my head. He's still observing himself pleasuring me. Our gazes meet in the mirror, and he brings his fingers to his mouth, savoring each one. "You taste absolutely divine." He speaks in a deep, husky tone. "I need more."

Our bodies glow golden in the light of the lamp.

His strong hands cup my breasts. With his eyes remaining on them through the mirror, he leans his mouth closer to my ear.

"Lie down and open your legs wide for me."

I crawl onto the bed and do as I'm told.

He's so hard for me, and his muscles flex as he positions himself between my knees, kissing the insides of my thighs. Unhurried, he fingers my swollen bud. His breaths are warm against my soaked sheath as he kisses it, short quick pecks, then...*Oh God*, his mouth cups my needy flesh and he sucks. I grind into it and buck my hips, yearning for more. "Oh, God," I cry out into the room. I peer down to see his head moving side to side as he sucks harder and faster, as though he hungers for me. I slide my fingers through his hair to glimpse more of his face, desiring to watch him pleasure me. He briefly glances up with a half-smile.

"Oh Silas, I'm there. Ohhh...Ohhh...Ohhh." I shout as my body shudders through a gratification I'm unsure I've ever known before. He moves his mouth down to my opening, drinking up every last bit of juice that flows from me.

Gradually, he kisses his way back up to my mouth, taking my hands and holding them over my head as he slides his thick flesh into me. "Your nectar is a rare delight," he groans into my ear. His plunges into me are unbelievably wonderful and I open my legs wider. "There you go, take it all in." His hands tighten on my wrists as he pounds harder.

I run my gaze over his broad shoulders and down his strong chest. His form is most striking. If my hands were free, I'd touch every inch of it.

"Oh, this has never felt so wonderful." He moves faster and harder. Our bodies are slick with sweat and my breasts bounce with each thrust of his hungry need. The flames of the lamp dance along the wall and up the ceiling. I peer down, watching him hammer in and out of me as my breath comes in tiny pants.

"Your breasts are making it hard to last much longer," he rasps staring down at them, then his body jolts and clenches as he moans out in pleasure.

A thrill radiates through me at the knowing I've done this to him.

Releasing my wrists, he draws me into his arms. Our breaths slowly return to normal as he lays kisses on my head.

Grabbing the blanket from the foot of the bed, he covers us. "My sweet Ginny," he hums, squeezing me tight.

"I never imagined having relations with a preacher would be that amazing," I murmur, burying my face in his warm chest.

"Do you imagine having relations with preachers often?"

I laugh. "I've never imagined having relations with a preacher, but if I had, I never would have imagined it'd be like that."

I prop myself up on my elbow to study his face. "Is it terrible to admit that I have imagined it with you since our first kiss? But still, I wondered if it would be foul. Unexciting."

"Foul and unexciting," he echoes, pulling me back into his chest. "It seems you thought little of me."

I laugh. "Clearly, I was incorrect."

"Well," he tips my chin and places a soft kiss on my lips. "I have much more to reveal to you."

The realization of our situation hits me, and I exhale in frustration. "Silas, we can't continue to sneak around."

"I know," he admits, tucking my hair behind my ear. "But I'm quite certain I can't live without you." He meets my mouth, and I give in to his touch, pushing thoughts of what comes next aside.

He nudges me to my back, taking my breast into his warm, wet lips.

"Turn over," he demands, and my body tingles at his words and sudden shift in his tone. I'm like wet clay in his hands. He can do as he wishes with me, and I'll mold myself into his will. "Put your rear in the air and spread your legs for me."

He smacks my backside. "You're an unruly girl, aren't you?" His voice is strong and authoritative.

I understand his intent.

"Yes," I whisper.

Another sting lands. "I didn't hear you." His hand meets my flesh again.

"Yes," I say louder.

I'm fully wanting more of this, more of him. He's rubbing his hard shaft between my wet thighs. "Do you know what?" There's another burn under his palm. "I like that you're an unruly girl." A sharp tingle dances over my skin. He pushes his hardness against my throbbing bud, and I tilt my backside up more so he can have full access to my soaked flesh. A slap echoes through the room with another gentle sting.

"You are an exquisite vision, my sweet Ginny." His voice is gravelly.

Guiding himself into me, he slowly smooths his calloused hand over my buttocks. Leisurely and deliberately, he glides his shaft into me, then he thrusts hard and deep. I meet his thrusts and tip my behind even more. I must have every inch of him.

"That's it." A hand runs up my back to my neck and into my hair, grabbing it taught. "That's it," he echoes, once more pounding into me while landing stinging blows to my backside.

Our movements reach a crescendo sparking our bodies to convulse in unison. Cries of pleasure mingle and fill the room before our breathless, sweating forms come to a halt and collapse upon the bed.

I topple onto my belly and Silas falls beside me tracing a finger over my rump.

"You're as red as a strawberry."

I smile at the thought of him marking me. I can't believe this mild-mannered man turns into an absolute beast during lovemaking, and I love it.

Silas kisses my shoulder. "I'm going to find a way for us to be together." Leaning in he lays his lips on my cheek. "I will never get enough of this," he moans.

I turn towards him as he draws me close. "Oh, Ginny. Sweet, sweet Ginny."

I grin as he squeezes me.

"I wish for you by my side every night," he whispers. "I don't want to live without you."

I inhale the scent of his skin, and the feeling of home wraps itself around me in a warm embrace. Wherever he is, is where I wish to be.

35

Silas

My day hasn't even begun and I'm already anxious to leave work. With quick steps, I make my way to the bank, which is still unfinished. *I must tell Ginny the truth.* As much as I desire to spend my life with her, it's not fair to ask her to marry me without her knowing the true me. Yes, I can step down as the preacher, and I shall. But still, I'll always know. I also must confess to Justus and Livvie. I have been such a fool to believe I could get away with this whole ruse, but I never imagined wishing to make this town my home, or finding true friends, or…falling in love.

As I round the corner of the feed mill, Milton Brady's voice is thunderous. "I don't know who Bennett thinks he is sending this man to my store." The man is pacing, face fiery red, while Samuel stands before him. I recall Justus sharing how Brady had refused once before to sell feed to Samuel.

"Aren't you a blacksmith on the Bennett Ranch? Why's it so important that you of all people come to my establishment and pick up his grain?"

I slow my pace, watching.

Samuel shifts from one foot to the other. "Mister Bennett is herding cattle today, sir, and he asked me to make the trip."

Brady continues to pace. "I don't like it. I don't like it one bit." He's shaking from anger.

This part of town is quieter, and it seems no one else is about, yet neither man takes note of me as I draw near.

Brady crosses his arms. "I just might not have that feed ready for three hours. You had best get back to the ranch. Bennett can come for it later."

Samuel speaks in a low tone. He's keeping his composure as he's been trained to do his whole life. Trained. My stomach wants to vomit my breakfast at the thought of this good man being treated so poorly.

"Speak up boy, I can't hear you," Brady shouts.

I've heard enough. Before I know it, I have the man's shirt collar wrapped up in my fist, shoving it into his throat. "Samuel is a grown man, and you will treat him as such. He is not a boy, and you will not refer to him as one. Do we have an understanding?"

Milton Brady's eyes bulge from his surprised face.

"Do we have an understanding?" I nudge him back as we're nose to nose.

He claws at my hand as he fights for air. He's not so fierce now.

I release his shirt but keep my eyes steady on him as he

backs away gasping for breath. "You've some nerve coming to my place of business and telling me how to run things. Over my dead body will I refer to this man as anything other than boy."

This man's hypocrisy makes my stomach turn and my fists ball at my sides.

I move nimbly around the ring as my opponent takes jabs at me. He is well aware that I'm undefeated, yet it is plain to see that his confidence borders on arrogance, and thinks he can best me. True, he has landed a few decent blows, but I allow him to believe he has a chance. It's a game of cat and mouse and I'm the cat.

"Come get me, mousy mousy mousy." I wave him towards me with my battered hand.

The room is sweltering and smells of hay and leather as sweat trickles down my back.

The crowd's shouting, "Flynn. Flynn. Flynn." Hearing my name fills me with the resolve to beat this scoundrel.

The other fighter — what is his name? Spentworth, yes, that's it. He delivers another blow to my face, and it pains me greatly, though I am accustomed to such discomfort. He shall have to do better than that. I continue to guard my midsection as he throws another strike at my head.

That's enough. I believe this crowd has witnessed all they need to. It's time for me to collect my earnings and depart from this place. I charge at him, and he retreats into the ropes as I land blow after blow until he clings to me for support. The referee intervenes and Spentworth collapses. My victory was assured, and once again, I've claimed it.

The men cheer, but unlike other fighters who prance around in victory, this means little to me. I step down from the ring, intent on collecting my winnings and leaving this town behind.

My mind comes back to Milton Brady who straightens his shirt in disgust, not knowing how seriously I could harm him.

"You will get this gentleman the feed Mister Bennett has sent him for, and you will do it with respect."

"I have no respect for this man," he spits. My arm draws back, and my fist meets his face.

He stumbles back with a howl, then examines his bloody hands. "You broke my nose."

My hands remain balled ready to strike again if I must. "Go get the man his feed before I break more than your nose."

"The church board will hear of this. You're done as this town's preacher."

A smile plays on my lips. "That's fine with me."

Brady turns towards the open doors of his building before giving a quick glance at Samuel, who has moved closer to my side, a stunned look upon his face. "Come get the bags and then leave my property at once."

I motion for Samuel to follow me as I make my way into the building to help haul the feed to the wagon. Pain throbs through my hand and I unclench and clench it a few times to make sure it too is not broken.

"Here, let us help." I notice my boss, Bart Matthews, with Calvin at his heels.

Calvin slaps my shoulder and chuckles. "We saw everything, Silas. I had no idea you had it in you."

"Ehhh, I've done a bit of boxing in my life." I shrug it off.

Bart chews on his cigar as usual. "I knew there was something different about you. What do you say you come to the saloon with me and the fellas at the end of the day?" He swings a bag of feed over his shoulder.

He has no idea how much I've missed the taste of whiskey on my tongue. "It appears I'm no longer the town preacher, so why not."

Bart lets out a hardy laugh.

"To Silas." The men raise their shot glasses. The liquid gives me that familiar burn down my throat and into my toes bringing me to life.

"Milton Brady has had that coming for years." Calvin pours us another shot from the bottle on the table.

"What will you do now?" asks George.

I down the shot and slam it on the table for a refill. "Well, if she'll have me, there's a girl I hope to marry."

Calvin pours whiskey into my glass. "What's her name?"

"Ginny."

Calvin lifts his glass, and the rest of us follow suit. "To Ginny."

"To Ginny." We say in unison before downing the spicy liquid.

Before I know it, I'm being supported by Calvin and George, my arms draped around them, as I can scarcely stand on my own.

"Don't take me to the parsonage," I slur.

"You can bunk with me," George says.

"But it's not even bedtime." Everything is spinning.

"My wife will prepare us a hearty meal."

"Will she be cross with you for bringing home a drunken

preacher?"

"No more cross than usual."

George and Calvin laugh.

Everyone we pass on the sidewalk is a blur. I try to focus my eyes but can't. I can't close them either in fear I'll be sick.

"Silas?"

I can't see her clearly, but I'd know that sweet voice anywhere.

"Ginny, my sweetheart." I remove my arms from George and Calvin to grab Ginny, but stumble into her instead.

"What in heaven's name is going on here?" she demands.

36

Ginny

The way Silas laid his hands and mouth upon my bare body is the only thing I've been able to think about since we were together yesterday evening. Goosebumps form over my skin at the thought of his touch. I don't know what his plan for us may be, but I have faith he has one.

Lenny nudges my arm. "What has you all smiles today?"

"What?" I realize I'm still grinning. I sigh.

"It's that preacher, isn't it?" She sinks heavily on the sofa and begins sewing a button to a pair of breeches.

I lay a blouse over the clothesline that runs the length of the room. "Perhaps."

"Not that it's any of my business, but you're my friend so I'm *making* it my business. How do you propose that a relationship with a preacher shall work out for you?"

I turn the crank while I feed a skirt through the wringer of the fine new machine that Lenny has purchased to ease the task of washing clothes. "I don't know, Len, but I believe I need to trust."

"Trust? Trust the preacher with carnal desires?" She gives me a wink.

"Yes," I state dramatically. "Believe me, his desires are more than mere lust, and he has assured me that he shall find a solution.

"Is he going to step down as the preacher? Or does he plan for you to be a preacher's wife? We both know you are not fit for that."

"I believe he will step down."

The water sloshes as I pull another skirt and crank it through the wringer. Having one of these machines would have been wonderful when I was laundering for the fellas. My hands would get so chapped and sore wringing clothing by hand. They'd take longer to dry as well. But these garments, there's not a drop of water left in them when I hang them on the line. Now that the weather is warmer, Lenny and I are able to open the windows and let in a cross breeze to dry them more quickly.

I'm just setting the iron atop the stove when the door bursts open and Livvie chuckles.

"Oh dear, I didn't mean to open it so harshly." She waddles in with Justus behind her. He closes the door gently while she takes a seat in the chair.

"Is it the baby?" Lenny comes to the edge of the sofa.

"No." Livvie glances at her protruding stomach as she smooths her hand over it. It sort of has the appearance of a watermelon.

Justus removes his hat. "I'm looking for Silas, and my bride insisted she come to town with me."

"I haven't seen him since last evening."

"We rode by the new bank site, but it appeared the men are all gone for the day, so we went to the parsonage, but he's not there either. We even checked the jail, but the sheriff said he had no reason to detain him that he knew of."

"Jail?" I wipe the sweat from my forehead with the back of my hand. "What would make you think to check the jail?"

"He broke Milton Brady's nose today defending Samuel." Justus smirks.

My hand shoots to my chest. *He what?* "He broke his nose? How? Why?"

"He punched him." The floor creaks under Justus's boots. "According to Samuel, Silas didn't care for the way Samuel was being treated by Brady. Silas insisted the man call Samuel by his name, rather than calling him boy, and when Brady refused…" Justus swipes his thumb over his nose and glances down towards his wife. "Well, he hauled off and landed a blow on Brady's face."

I know Silas to be a good man, and I'm proud of him for standing up for Samuel, who is equally a man of good character. "Good for him." I rest my hands on my hips deciding what to do next. Livvie's leaned back in the chair cradling her swollen belly.

Lenny lays her needlework to the side. "What happened then?"

"As Samuel tells it, Bart Matthews and another man walked up from the road and helped Silas and Samuel load the wagon with the feed I'd sent him there to purchase."

I remembered Justus saying he would no longer buy from Milton Brady if he gave Samuel anymore trouble. "Does this mean you'll be looking for a new seller to purchase your feed from?"

"Indeed, it does. I may have to make larger, though less frequent, purchases, but that man has lost my business." Justus rubs his chin. "I have had another thought as well."

Livvie cranes her neck to peer up at him. "What thought is that?"

He gives her a sly grin. "I just might start my own feed store and send ole Milton Brady right out of business."

She cocks a brow. "How would you do that?"

He gives the tip of her turned-up nose a playful tap with his finger. "I'm a resourceful man, Angel."

Lenny crosses the room to place a shirt with the remaining finished work for the day. "You two are quite the pair, simply too charming."

"Yes, they are." I stare at my pregnant friend and her handsome husband. I wonder if this could ever be me and Silas. *Oh, Silas, where are you?*

"Did you check the McCalister's?" I ask.

Justus takes his attention from Livvie. "Yes, they haven't seen him, but made it clear in no uncertain terms that when I find him, I am to see to it that he is moved out of the parsonage immediately."

Heat roils in my stomach. "For defending an innocent man?"

"That's not how they perceive it. To them, their preacher has struck against an elder of the church."

I cross my arms then place them back on my hips as I pace the small spot where I'm standing. "That's goddamn horseshit."

"That is goddamn horseshit," Lenny echoes.

"I would agree with you ladies." Justus tucks a wayward strand of hair behind Livvie's ear.

I groan. "Well, Lenny, I'll finish this tomorrow. I must see if I can help find Silas."

He's most likely riddled with guilt for what he's done.

Go home. A voice calls to me.

I can't go home. I have to find Silas. The urge to grasp the stone around my neck is overwhelming. I press my hand to my chest, feeling its weight through my blouse.

Go home.

"Justus, would you mind giving me a ride to Doc and Miss Bea's?"

"Certainly." Justus helps Livvie to her feet.

As the horses pull the wagon down the main street my heart is so heavy over Silas. What does this all mean for him and for us?

Suddenly, Justus tugs at the reins. "Whoa." The wagon stops in the middle of the road.

Livvie grabs his arm. "What are you doing, Justus Bennett?"

"I believe we have just found our man."

When my eyes follow the direction Justus motions to, I see a slumped and stumbling Silas being helped down the sidewalk by two men.

"Oh, for heaven's sake," I mumble, hopping from the seat.

37

Silas

I wake to my head pounding and the room spinning. Moving my tongue about within my mouth, I will moisture to appear, yet it remains as dry as the desert floor. *Water.* It's been a long while since I've known this kind of craving. The only thing that competes with my need for water is my need to use the privy. Rolling to the side of the bed, I realize I'm not in my bed or in my room, then I remember George offering to take me to his house.

Shoving my feet into my boots, I notice the blue and pink hues of the morning sky as the sun makes its way over the horizon. *I'm on the Bennett Ranch.* The house is quiet, and I tiptoe down the hall, making my way to the outhouse. It feels strange to be in the most intimate parts of Justus and Livvie's home. As I approach the stairs, the scent of bacon and coffee greet me and my stomach churns with hunger.

Unsure of who's in the kitchen, and not wanting to show my

guilty face just yet, I decide to slip out the front door.

"Good morning, Reverend." Mary startles me just as I reach for the doorknob.

Mary and her husband Frank have lived on the ranch since Justus was a boy. Frank helps as a ranch hand and Mary cooks and cleans for the main house. Justus always speaks about how Mary has been like a ma to him since his own died when he was a teen.

Their son Caleb still lives with them, but he's set to marry Adelyn Chastain, a recent divorcee with a child, this fall.

I squeeze my eyes closed. Mary is the last person I wanted to see. I love her, but I don't know how she will receive me in my current state.

"Good morning, Mary." I give her my widest, although pasty smile.

She wipes her hands on her apron. "Are you leaving us so soon?"

"No, just going to use the privy."

"You do know there's a water closet upstairs?"

Although I knew the Bennetts had one of those, I'm not one to snoop about looking for it. "Getting a bit of fresh air shall do me good."

"Ah, yes. Well, Justus has already eaten and gone out to do chores. Come to the kitchen for breakfast after you mind your business."

I extend my hand towards the knob once more. "I'll do that. Thank you, Mary."

Once I've used the privy, I head for the pump, greedily drinking handfuls of cold crisp water before scrubbing my face with it and running my wet fingers through my hair. The morning air is chilly and frost smoke hovers over the field.

I consider heading for the barn, but my stomach begs for food, so I decide to face Mary instead.

Staring out the big picture window at the kitchen table, I sip my coffee and watch as the sky turns a pale blue and the sun burns off the fog. I received no questions or judgment from Mary as she heaped my plate with food then left me to eat in silence.

It appears today is the day of reckoning. At the thought, I sit my mug down and rest my forehead against my fist. *Where do I start?*

"You know it's not good manners to have your elbows on the table."

I flinch at Ginny's playful words.

Ginny.

Rising from the table, I almost knock over the chair. "Ginny. I didn't know you were here."

She pours herself a cup of coffee. "I stayed in another spare room."

I desperately wish to wrap my arms around her.

Sitting beside me she sips from her mug. "You want to tell me what happened yesterday?"

I open and close my hand, studying the swollen knuckles. The image of Milton Brady's smug face fills my mind. "I just couldn't stand there and listen to Brady treat Samuel as if he were no better than a dog."

She places her hand over mine, gently caressing her thumb over my fingers. "That part I know and understand. I'm proud of you for standing up for Samuel."

My heart warms at her words. The morning light smooths her skin and makes her eyes shine like gems. I have an urge to take hold of her braid, pull her towards me, and greedily kiss her beautiful mouth.

She sits back and takes another sip. "The part I don't understand is finding you so drunk off your feet from too much whiskey." An eyebrow rises but there's no judgment or disappointment in her statement.

"Bart and Caleb saw what happened with Milton and believed I did an admirable thing. They, with the rest of the men I work with, offered to take me for a drink after we'd finished for the day, and I agreed."

"Why would you agree to that? Have you ever drunk spirits in your life?"

I stare down at my half-eaten plate of food and run my hands over the thighs of my breeches. "There's a lot about me you don't know." My stomach turns as I believe this is perhaps the beginning of the end.

"Well, I believe this is as good a time as any to inform me of all I don't know." She crosses one arm over the other and settles into her chair.

I shove my fingers through my hair and watch Buck run around one of the ranch hands down by the barn as the man swings a bucket from his fingers.

"For starters, I need to confess to Justus and Livvie that their marriage may not be legally binding."

"What do you mean my marriage may not be legally binding?" Livvie stands in the doorway, her hand resting on her swollen belly.

38

Ginny

I rush to Livvie, dumbstruck at the revelation that her marriage might not be legal. "Come sit. I'll pour you coffee. It appears Silas has *much* explaining to do." I glare at him over my shoulder.

I'm doing my best to remain calm for Livvie's sake, but inside my stomach is tied up in knots. *Who is this man that I've fallen in love with?* I'm fearful to find out.

Silas pushes his plate away. "I believe Justus ought to be here for this conversation."

"And I believe you ought to tell me right now, Silas Flynn, why my husband is not my husband." Livvie taps a finger on the table with each word.

"Livvie, I'm truly sorry. I need you to first believe that. I never intended for anyone to get hurt."

I hand Livvie her coffee and take Silas's plate from the table.

"I'm not entirely the person you've believed me to be."

He runs his hand along the scruff of his face. "I wish it were possible to turn back time and arrive in this town under more favorable circumstances."

My heart races. "What do you mean?"

His eyes are pained and pleading. "To begin, I'm not a preacher. I've never been a preacher."

"Which is why you believe my marriage not to be legal." Livvie stares out the window.

I wish I knew her thoughts.

"What's your real name?" I demand.

"My name is Silas Flynn. That's the truth."

"How did you come to find yourself living this life of deception here in Laurel Springs as the *virtuous* town minister?" I fold my arms across my chest, swallowing past the lump in my throat.

Silas mimics my posture by sitting back and crossing his arms. "I've always been a bit of a nomad, never living anywhere for long. I believed Laurel Springs to be no different."

My lip quivers. "How many people have you hurt along the way? How many other hearts have you shattered? How many women have you tricked?"

He straightens and reaches across the table as if I'm going to take his hand. I remain still. "Please, you must believe me. I've never cared for any woman as I do you. You're the reason I stayed. I've been seeking a way to set this right." He lowers his head. "I've failed miserably."

Tapping my foot, I glance to Livvie, who glares at Silas as though she's trying to figure him out. "Let's hear the rest of your story." Her tone is calmer than the storm that rages within me.

"My father wasn't a kind man. He abused my mother and drank every day except Sunday. Sundays were the days he was a good Christian man."

Silas chuckles. "He helped construct the church building. He'd even give Widow Dillon rides to church every Sunday morning. Anything she needed he was there to help. She believed him to be a saint."

"One day I walked into the house with the morning's milk pail for my ma and he had her by the back of the head, hair tangled in his fist." Silas's hand clenches as to mimic his father's action.

"'Please, James, you're hurting me,' she cried. Her hands were behind her head holding his arm, from the pain no doubt."

"I lived with this my whole life. My father abusing me and my mother. My brothers, who are much older than me, moved out around 16 years of age and never returned. I could always see that it caused my ma great pain to lose her sons due to her husband."

The sound of boots brings my attention to the doorway of the kitchen where Justus stands. He leans against the frame and folds his arms.

Silas continues as if lost in the past.

"Father had Ma's face near the frying pan, threatening to mar her for the remainder of her life, because she burned the bacon. I realized she was attempting to keep her head from the sizzling grease."

"In all his rage, the man didn't notice me, or if he did, he didn't care. I'd had enough of his bullying. Something came over me and I ran back out the door, throwing the pail of milk and grabbing a large rock. It fit nicely in my hand."

Silas emulates holding a rock in his palm the way he must have done long ago.

"He had my mother's head turned back with her face in his. She was bent at an odd angle. Spittle flew into her eyes that brimmed with tears of pain and fear. His back was mostly to me, although if he had been in his right mind, he'd surely have seen me out of the corner of his eye, coming at him with that stone. I hit him on the head. Stunned, he let go of her. I struck again, not giving him an opportunity to defend himself or take the rock from me. He grabbed his head where I hit him, then he peered down at the blood covering his hand. I couldn't conceive why he was still standing there. And Ma was shrieking, 'Silas, no.' But I hit him once more and he tumbled to the floor. All the disdain I'd felt my entire life for this man poured out through that rock onto his head over and over."

Tears run down Silas's face.

"Ma was still screaming, but now she was attempting to pull me from him. I couldn't stop." Silas stifles a chuckle. "There was a sense of contentment in that. It felt just. Finally, exhaustion and brokenness took over and I stopped. The man was dead. He was dead. I rose and the stone fell to the floor with a thud. The only sound then was that of my heavy breaths and the blood pounding in my ears."

He folds his hands and bows his eyes.

"When I peered over my shoulder my ma stood with her hands to her mouth. A look of horror was plainly written over her face. Her eyes moved from him to me, back to him, then to me. I was terrified that she feared me. Or worse, that she abhorred me. I couldn't imagine what she was thinking, except that she was clearly aghast."

"With her eyes on my father, she held out a shaky hand to me, as if calling me to her but frightened he'd get up and attack us. 'Silas,' she whispered."

"She was reaching for me, so I took her hand. 'We must take care of his body.' She was trembling. All sense had come to me then, and I noticed the bacon was still on the stove. Smoke from the grease of the pan filled the room and stung my eyes."

"'Go outside, Ma. I'll take care of this,' I told her as I grabbed the iron pan with a cloth and tossed it outside onto the grass."

"I took my father's body, in the back of the wagon, to an old well on our property and filled it with his body and his beloved rocks. We told everyone that he left for Chicago and never returned. It was known that my father was prone to drink, so no questions were asked further about him."

"My ma was so concerned about the blood on my hands and the fact that I'd spend all of eternity burning in hell that she insisted I leave to live with my brother Jody and attend seminary school, as if that would mend everything."

"She wrote to Jody and told him Father had left us. It wasn't a falsehood, but it wasn't the full truth either. Jody came and retrieved us and our belongings to live with him and his family."

Silas glances between me and Livvie.

"Shortly after arriving at my brother's, I discovered he and I didn't see eye to eye, so one night I wrote my mother a note of apology, packed what I could in my bag, and left. I felt no regret in leaving her, for I no longer feared for her well-being, knowing that Jody would care for her as she deserved. She smiled more than I'd ever seen her smile and a youthfulness I'd never noticed lit her face. She was free. Freedom, what a sweet word."

He releases a loud exhale.

"While the Confederates launched their attack on Fort Sumter, I was boarding a ship for Ireland. By happenstance, General Lee's army surrendered on the very day I set foot back upon American soil."

Livvie clutches her mug. "Silas, I'm so sorry that happened to you."

Justus's boots clomp across the floor as he makes his way towards Silas.

39

Silas

I'm jolted from my recollection by a firm hand upon my shoulder. I peer up to see Justus standing above me.

"I'm sorry you went through that."

I nod. "Thank you."

Livvie pats the table. "Come have a seat, Justus. Silas has more to share."

I rub my hands together. Ginny hasn't said a word. She remains still with her watery eyes brimming and her hands to her lips.

I continue. "I've traveled all across this land working and resting my head wherever I was able. For a time, I earned a fair sum as a bareknuckle boxer."

Justus perks up. "A boxer. You don't say?"

"One evening, I found myself caught in a brawl at a pub in Ireland, where I managed to fend off three men. After witnessing the altercation, a fellow named Stephen suggested I had a knack for it. When he mentioned the earnings, I decided it might be worth a try."

Justus takes Livvie's hand and gives her a wink.

"Turns out, I am a natural at boxing. I could make the money last a while, but eventually I'd return when the coins in my purse ran low."

I smile to Ginny with hopes to relieve her concerns. She wipes the tears from her face, and I continue.

"In time I grew weary of the constant blows." I open and close my swollen hand. "I was tired of hitting."

Justus clears his throat. "When did you decide to become a preacher?"

My heart sinks. "I'm afraid you missed that part. As I was recalling to the ladies, I didn't." I sit up straighter and let out a breath before looking my friend in the eye. "I'm not a preacher, Justus."

Justus leans forward, sits his elbow on the table, and runs his hand over his beard and stares at me.

"I'm afraid you and Livvie don't have a legally binding marriage."

I rub my sweaty palms against one another.

Justus smirks. "No, we are legally married. It's been recorded in the county registry, which is all that is required in this county. Besides…" Justus reaches for his wife's hand. "I don't need the law to tell me this angel's my wife."

Livvie's face radiates with joy as she gazes at Justus while caressing her belly.

Ginny appears as though she may be ill.

"As I was telling Livvie and Ginny, Justus, I didn't mean to cause anyone pain. I never intended to remain in Laurel Springs. But then I met you and the Peterson's and began falling in love with this town." I glance at Ginny. "When I met Ginny, I knew I was ready to finally settle down."

Our gaze locks in an intense stare.

"How did you manage to get away with this? Coming to town as the new preacher? I know they were expecting a minister, but I assume he wasn't you. What happened to him?" Justus sits back and places a hand on his thigh.

"Reverend George Brown." I shake my head. "I met him on a train bound for Omaha. He was a terrible man—boisterous, ate with his fat fingers, boastful. He had been bragging that the seminary school was sending him to the territories to save the heathens from hell. He believed everyone in the territories to be whores and thieves."

Livvie gasps.

"I didn't care for him, but beyond that I didn't think much of him."

I trace the lines in the grain of the wood on the table with my finger. "Unfortunately, I had to room with the man at the boarding house where we stayed. To help me tolerate living with him for the remainder of the three days until he was to depart, I went and bought myself a bottle of whiskey to sneak back to my room. The lady who ran the establishment didn't allow liquor."

"Upon returning to the house, I heard a young lady crying from the dark shadows between the homes, begging for someone to stop. I must be honest that I didn't believe it my business, but then I heard that fat bastard's voice."

"When I came upon them his breeches were around his knees, and he had her held against the house. He was growling that he had the authority by God to take what he wanted if she didn't give it to him."

Recalling Livvie's story of being raped by her stepfather which resulted in a pregnancy that ended in abortion, I decide to go no further with my explanation of this man's horrendous actions towards the girl.

"He charged at me with a rock and that's when I hit him over the head with my whiskey bottle, killing him. He won't be hurting any more young ladies."

Justus shifts in his seat. "I'll say."

"I saw something glistening white in the moonlight, so I snatched it up and stuck it in my pocket. After sending the young woman on her way with the promise she'd never repeat a word of what happened, I snuck back to my room. Needless to say, the letter, which Brown carried with him from the school, was in rough condition, but the McCalisters took my word as you could still make out the seminary's logo and the signature of the school's president. Although smudged from whiskey and mud, much of the wording was still visible, save for George Brown's name."

Livvie shakes her head in disbelief. "I'm so thankful you stopped that man from harming the girl."

"Didn't the church know George Brown and not Silas Flynn was to be coming to town?" Justus narrows his eyes.

"As George Brown indicated, the board of the Laurel Springs

church sent a letter to the seminary, requesting that they send a preacher. George was entrusted with delivering the letter from the school, confirming that he had indeed been sent by them. By some fortunate stroke of luck, which I might add, I did purposely use to my advantage, the missive was partially damaged, and the board never raised a question about its authenticity."

Justus wags a finger at me. "I always knew there was something peculiar about you."

I glance at each one of them—Livvie, Justus, and Ginny—peering into their eyes. "I truly am sorry for misleading you all. I love you three, more than anyone, besides my ma. And…" I fold my hands on the table and study them. "The lives I've taken haunt me every day. I only did what I had to do, to protect others." I look to Ginny, willing her to comprehend.

"I would wager Justus understands." Livvie gives her husband a sad smile.

Justus nods. "Indeed I do."

Ginny shoots up out of the chair and runs to the door leading outdoors from the kitchen. "I don't know that I can do this," she murmurs.

40

Ginny

I'm unsure if I even closed Livvie's kitchen door behind me. I don't know where I'm going, I just lift my skirts and run. The sun is warm, and the scent of hay and manure calms my senses as I near the pasture and drop into the grass. My world is spinning, and I don't know how to make it stop.

The sky is a light blue with wisps of clouds.

"Why, Jake? Why did you leave me? Our life was so simple. I trusted you. Why?" I bury my face in my hands and sob.

I don't want to live like this. I don't want to live without you, Jake. We were a perfect pair, like jam on toast.

If he hadn't died, we'd still be living our beautiful life together. Surely, we'd have a child by now—perhaps two or three. I had such hopes to have Jake's babies. We'd daydream about it together all the time. But there was one day that almost broke us.

The sun shone through the flap of the wagon cover directly into my eyes. It's the first I'd seen the sun in days as it has been one storm after another. We sat up camp here the afternoon before because the horses needed rest from clopping through mud and hail. This is the most sheltered spot we could find.

I roll over to snuggle into Jake's arms, but he's gone. He's always been an early riser, but occasionally a husband can surprise his wife and do something unexpected, like stay in bed longer than usual.

I dress and descend from the wagon to discover Jake has a fire burning and coffee boiling. He gazes out over the horizon discussing the day's plans with Mark Masterson, another one of the men in the wagon train. Mark and his family plan to go ahead to Oregon, while Jake believes the Colorado territory would be best for us.

I run my hand over my slightly swollen stomach, wishing to wrap my arms around my husband and tell him good morning. Only Greta Masterson knows I'm with child. It has been hard for pregnant women, the journey over the Great Plains, through rivers, up and down embankments, and during a beating sun and angry rainstorms. I don't wish anyone to look at me with sad eyes, or disgruntled ones either for that matter. With any luck, we'll reach Colorado before the baby is born.

Two children have died on the trip, and my only hope and prayer is that ours makes it safely.

"I suppose we better get some food in this belly," I quietly say to our little one who grows inside me. I find a few small potatoes and sit upon a log that Jake laid before the fire, like a bench, big enough for the two of us. I set to dicing them. I'm thinking fried potatoes and the little salt pork we have left, with coffee, should do just fine this morning,

especially since my appetite is returning. I was terribly ill for a while there, which didn't begin until after we started the journey West. I had never considered becoming pregnant on this trip.

Our food supply has been low for a couple of weeks. We lost our flour and sugar while crossing a flooded river. If we had flour, I could make biscuits or pancakes, perhaps. Concerns are growing in the camp, and fights have broken out amongst the leaders.

"Ginny, goot morning." Greta, my new German friend, waves to me from their campsite as two-year-old Able Masterson runs towards our fire. I'm so frightened he'll trip and fall right into it that I set the pan of potatoes on the ground and leap towards him. Just as I do, I feel a pain I've never experienced before, worse than any monthly pain. Able stops, places two fingers in his mouth, and stares up at me with big round blue eyes as I hunch over, grabbing my stomach and crying out.

Jake spins and looks my way then runs and grabs me. He guides me back to the log, but the pain is unbearable.

"Get her in ze vagon," Greta states. "Al tend tuh her."

I writhe in pain all that day and into the night. The wagon train is due to leave the next morning. There's talk of Fort Kearney being a week away, and although we desperately need to restock our supplies, Jake insists we won't move until I am well enough to do so.

"I'm losing the child, aren't I?" I cry as I lay curled up in a ball holding my stomach in agony.

Greta dabs my sweat-soaked forehead with a cool rag. "Shhh, nah don't zay sooch tings." Her German accent is thick on her tongue.

"I fear I'm losing the child. I'm certain of it." I turn my head away from her and weep.

When dusk falls, I hear the dreaded words from Greta, "Yoo have too poosh, Ginny."

I don't want to push. I've been fighting the urge for hours. I've felt my body attempting to rid itself of the baby, but I can't bear it.

"Pleeze, yoo moost poosh. Yake needz yoo. And, ze pain vill seeze."

She's right and I'm in so much pain I don't believe I can fight it any longer. I push, bearing down, my face tight. Taking another inhale, I push once more, squeezing my knees to my chest. Again, I push, releasing a loud scream, and something slips from me.

I lay back and cry as Greta wraps the contents in cloth.

"Please, I need to see."

She holds it against her chest. "Yoo don't vant too zee."

"I must," I say firmly, reaching towards her.

She nods and passes the bundle to me. I open the bloody rag and inside is an unformed being. There are eyes, stubs for arms and legs with little buds for the hands and feet. Its oddly shaped head glistens in the light of the lamp.

I am so consumed with my grief I hardly notice Greta washing me. When she finishes, she tucks blankets around me and smooths my hair from my face. "Al go get Yake."

Jake approaches cautiously, crawling towards me to peer at our little one that I hold in my hand, wrapped in the same blood-soaked cloth.

He sniffles, catching my attention and causing me to look up at him.

"Oh, Ginny, I'm so sorry. I'm so sorry." He buries his head in my hair and sobs. He wraps his arms around me and together we weep.

I wake and as usual, Jake is gone. Maybe it was all just a terrible dream. But, no. The unformed child lay beside me. It is terribly and unforgettably real. The sounds of voices, neighing of horses, and chopping of wood fill my ears. Life is going on outside of our little wagon despite the loss inside.

"Ginny?" Jake calls softly as he peers around the canvas of the wagon.

"I'm awake."

He climbs in and kisses me. "The wagon train's pulling out in an hour with or without us. I believe it's best we stay together."

I nod and wipe fresh tears from my cheek.

I tap a box beside me. "This one, will you pull it out and take my jewelry box?"

"Ginny, this is no time for concerning yourself with trinkets."

"It's for the baby. It'll fit in it nicely. I'll cut a piece of gingham to lay inside."

Without another word, Jake begins moving boxes until he reaches the one with my jewelry case.

As I make a lovely little bed for our baby, the scraping sound of Jake's shovel meets my ears. The reality hits me like a stray ball and a fresh wave of tears spill. I'll never be able to visit this grave, never able to speak with him or her. I won't be able to lay fresh flowers at the cross come spring and summer.

Jake helps me from the wagon as I cradle the box in my skirts so that it doesn't slip and fall, then I place it gently down in the deep hole that my husband dug beneath a hickory tree.

Jake holds me while I sing the only song I know to sing to a baby, "Can You Count the Stars." I loved hearing Greta sing it to little Able in German so much that she has taught it to me in English, to sing to our child.

Can you count the stars that brightly
twinkle in the midnight sky?
Can you count the clouds, so lightly

o'er the meadows floating by?
God, the Lord, doth mark their number,
with His eyes that never slumber;
He hath made them everyone.

When the song has ended, Jake softly kisses my cheek, then scoops the dirt into the hole, atop the little box that now holds our sweet child. Then he fashions a cross from two sticks and places it at the head of the grave.

I know Jake blamed himself for our loss, but I never once blamed him. It was a decision we made together, and now I know Jake's with her, and she's not truly remaining beneath a hickory tree after all.

The crunch of dry grass under boots grows louder and I sense Silas approaching me from behind. Buck trots over and nuzzles my arm seeking loving pets. Silas sits, ankles crossed, knees raised with his elbows propped upon them.

I give all my attention to Buck, not wishing to acknowledge the man before me at this moment.

"Are you going to keep on ignoring me?"

My stomach sinks at his question, and I swallow back tears that threaten to spill if I dare open my mouth.

He drops his knees and fingers the cloth of my skirt.

I wish desperately to say something, but all I can do is stare down at a relaxed Buck. The grasses sway in the breeze, and the sun is like a warm kiss upon my face.

"I'm sorry about a lot of things, Ginny, but the one thing I won't apologize for is falling in love with you." He scans the yard then hangs his head. "If you'll never have me again, I'll never regret the memories I have of you. Of us. I don't lament a moment of it."

A faint scent of something sweet tickles my nose. A flower of some sort.

"Silas?" It's all I can manage to say. How do I show vulnerability here, now?

"Listen, Ginny." He places his hand upon my leg.

I lay my hand over his. "No, Silas, let me, please."

"All right." His eyes meet mine.

"This is all confusing and emotional and scary. I've been afraid that being with you means I'll forget about Jake. The moment I decide to let you in…" I lay my hand over my heart. "I don't know that I can trust you anymore."

He moves closer and takes both of my hands in his. "Ginny, I'm so sorry I deceived you, that I deceived everyone. I wasn't expecting to make friends and fall in love. I'm unsure at what point it would have been a good time for me to confess, but I have now. All my sins are out to those I love and care about the most." He takes my chin in his hand. "One thing I can reassure you of is I've never desired anything more in my life than I do you."

How I wish to fall into his arms. Get lost in his eyes. Place my mouth against his. Every carnal need a woman could ever imagine, I have it now and I'm fighting with all my being, but I cannot live with a man I don't know.

"I'm sorry, Silas." I gently shake Buck letting him know to move so I can stand. "I need some time."

Silas jumps to his feet. "Let me walk you back to the house."

I stop and turn but do not dare to look at him. "No. Please."

41

Silas

I leave the ranch shortly after Ginny, contemplating what will transpire when I arrive at the parsonage to pick up my few belongings. Where I'll live now, I don't know, but I'm certain I have enough money to stay at the hotel for a short time.

Justus lent me a gelding that he said needs to be returned to Clint. This will save him a trip to town. The livery will be my first stop, and I ponder confessing to Clint, if he doesn't already know.

I sway on the back of the horse with every ache in my heart. I have no choice but to be a man. Ginny made it clear we're over. The question is, do I remain in Laurel Springs, or do I move on? This has been a struggle I've wrestled with for almost the last year that I've been here.

Numbness settles into my soul. The plodding of hooves is all I sense. Then I'm jolted out of my thoughts by the neighing of the horse Ginny left the ranch on. I jump off from the gelding and take the whinnying horse by the reins.

"Where's Ginny, boy?" I glance around. "Ginny," I call. "Ginny, where are you?" The white of her blouse and blonde of her hair stands out as she lay in the grass off the road. "Ginny!" I rush to her, but she's not conscious. Her head is bleeding, and the crimson liquid stains a large rock. Lifting her over my horse I hold tight both to her and the second horse as I ride to town as quickly as I am able.

"I have you, sweetheart." I kiss her head that's cradled in my arm. "I'm taking you to Doc as quickly as I can."

Her arms hang limp, bouncing with the movement of the animal.

"Git." I nudge the horse in the side to move along faster, traveling on the outskirts of town because the main street will slow me down. Once I reach Doc's, I carry Ginny in, not bothering to knock.

"Doc, Miss Bea, anyone?" I yell out. Hopelessness suffocates me. "Please be home."

"Goodness, Silas." Miss Bea's eyes fall upon Ginny and her hands go to her mouth in a startled gasp.

Doc appears in the doorway removing his spectacles. "What's happened?" He guides me to lay Ginny upon the cot in his exam room.

"I found her lying near the road on my way back from the ranch. Her horse was in hysterics. I believe she fell or was bucked off. Her head was near a large rock."

"Oh goodness." Miss Bea moves about the room.

"Ahhh, yes, she has quite the bump here where she's bleeding. I'll need to clean and stitch this up."

"Yes, dear." Miss Bea frantically grabs items from the drawers of the bureau.

"We'll take good care of her, Reverend." Doc pats my shoulder.

I back away towards the door with my eyes remaining upon Ginny. "Do you mind if I sit out here and wait?"

Miss Bea chimes in. "Oh, no sense in waiting around here." She looks at me as if I haven't bathed in weeks. "Go home and get yourself cleaned up." I run my hand over my whiskered face and glance down at my shirt. Blood. Ginny's blood stains the front of me. I nod and see myself out.

I took the horses back to the livery. A young boy helped me with the return, so I never saw Clint. I had hoped to be as fortunate when I went to the parsonage to fetch my belongings. Poor Naomi was meowing up a storm when she met me at the back steps. I'm certain she missed me, and I felt a great sense of guilt for her being trapped in here for so long.

Thankfully I did not happen upon anyone before returning to the Peterson's with Naomi in hand.

"I came to check on Ginny."

Miss Bea gives me a sad look. "I'm afraid she hasn't woken yet, poor dear."

"May I see her? Do you think she could hear me if I speak to her?"

"Well, I don't see how it could hurt. Come with me."

I follow Miss Bea down the hall and up the stairs. "We put her back in her own bed so when she wakes, she feels comfortable."

A loud thump followed by Ginny's screams startle us. "Oh, God. Where am I? Where am I? I can't see. Someone help me. Help me." Her cries are blood curdling.

I drop the cat, and run for Ginny.

"Ginny dear, it's Miss Bea. It's all right." She grabs the girl to calm her, but Ginny's arms are flailing about in a frenzy.

"I can't see. Oh, God, you must help me. I can't see." She moves quickly about the room and stumbles over the bed and falls. "Someone help me. I can't breathe. Anybody. Where's Doc? Please." She reaches out but her hands grasp at air.

I take her arm. "Ginny, sweetheart, it's Silas. Let me help you."

"Silas." She claws at me in a desperate attempt to leave the darkness that entraps her. "Where's Doc? Please."

Miss Bea and I give each other a knowing look before she leaves the room.

"Ginny, please, let's get you back in bed. You had a fall and now you're at Doc and Miss Bea's. It's going to be all right."

She clings to me as her eyes dart about. "Help me, please. It's so dark, Silas. It's so dark." Her breaths are quick and shallow. "I can't breathe," she cries.

I hold her close. "Deep breaths, sweetheart. Take deep breaths. You must calm yourself."

She pushes away from me. "No. I have to get out of here." She stumbles and her arms splay as her eyes search for sight. "This can't be happening. I can't live like this." She unbuttons the collar of her blouse.

"Ginny, please." I reach for her gently. "Please stay close to me so you don't fall and hurt yourself. Let's go back to the bed."

"I don't want to lay in bed. Don't you understand? I want to see, goddamn it," she shouts. Her hair and eyes are wild.

"I know, sweetheart." I reach for her again, but she slaps my hand away.

"Don't *sweetheart* me. I want to see." She shrinks back to the floor in a heap and sobs. "I just want to see."

I move to my knees and pull her to me. "I know," I say past the soreness in my throat.

Doc's footsteps move close. "Ginny, I want you to take this medicine. It will help you."

She lifts her head, still crying, she wipes at her face. "Will it help me see?"

"Come on now, dear," says Miss Bea. "Let's get you to the bed so you can take the medicine."

She allows me and Miss Bea to help her to the bed where Doc gives her the concoction to drink.

"This shall help you sleep," he says after she swallows it down.

"Please." She tugs at his arm. "Don't leave me. Don't leave me alone," she cries.

"I can stay." I glance between Doc and Miss Bea. "If you're all right with that, Ginny."

Her eyes dart about. "Yes." She stretches her arms, reaching for me. My heart breaks at the sight of her. "I'm right here." I take her hand and sit on the side of the bed.

"The rocker's in the corner, dear," Miss Bea says, then she and Doc leave the room.

Ginny closes her eyes. "I'm scared. You promise not to leave me? You'll be here when I wake up?"

"I promise." I smooth her hair and kiss her forehead.

"I'm sorry," she says drowsily.

"Shhh. Just rest." I take her hand in both of mine and kiss her fingers.

Lying beside Ginny, I stroke her hair as she sleeps. I can't help but reflect on life and my thoughts about God. Why would He allow this to happen to her? Anger bubbles in me at the unfairness of it all. The anger continues to build, and I get up and go to the window. "How could you do this to her?" I grit out to God. If there is a God. "How?" I pace the room and shake my fists to the ceiling. "Take my sight, damn it. If you want to hurt someone, hurt me. You hear me? Take my eyes. Take my tongue and my arms and legs while you're at it." My chest heaves. I fall to my knees and weep. "Take *my* eyes."

After a moment of silent rage, I compose myself, taking the chair from the corner and moving it to the side of the bed. I wipe my face with my sleeves and push my hair back. When I look up, Ginny's eyes are open.

"Ginny?" I sit beside her.

"I heard you."

I choke back a cry.

"I still can't see." She says it with a calmness I can't comprehend. "My sight won't return, will it?"

Bile stings the back of my throat, and I swallow it down.

"Doc says time shall tell. Do you remember what happened?"

"Something frightened the horse. I don't know if I don't recall what scared it, or if I didn't see it. I tried to hold onto his reins. That's the last I can recollect."

I caress the back of her hand and lay soft kisses upon it. The urge to open my chest and shelter her safely inside is overwhelming.

"I found you lying off in the grass. You hit your head on a rock. Busted it wide open. I brought you here as quickly as I could, and Doc cleaned your wound and stitched it up."

"It hurts." Her eyes stare into a void.

"Do you need me to go get him?" I continue to hold her hand close to my face.

She grabs for me in a panic. "No. Don't leave me."

"It's all right," I soothe. "I won't go."

"Who's there?" Ginny asks just as Livvie's presence fills the doorway.

"I came as soon as I heard," Livvie whispers, moving slowly and cautiously toward the bed.

"Oh, Livvie." Ginny begins to cry and holds out her arms, not completely sure where her friend is.

Livvie sits on the other side of the bed and embraces her. "What can I do?"

"Just hold me."

They cry together and I watch with a helplessness that drowns me.

Once their tears are shed and faces wiped, Livvie looks to me but speaks to Ginny. "Silas appears worse than he did at the ranch. Why don't I stay the night with you so he can go clean up and rest?"

Ginny holds Livvie's hand. "I can't ask you to stay the night away from Justus."

Livvie slides her fingers over Ginny's braid. "He and I will have plenty more nights together."

"Silas?" Ginny reaches for me, not quite in the right direction.

"I'm here." I take her hand.

"Are you all right with Livvie staying with me?"

"I can't say I'm pleased to leave you, but I suppose I could use some rest and a bath. I'll be back tomorrow after work if that's all right."

I look to Livvie. "I'll be staying at the hotel if you need me." I move from the bed. "I just need to find Naomi first."

"Oh, please bring her to me when you do. Let her stay with me, will you?"

I stare at my sweetheart and smile, recalling her love of animals. "Of course I will."

I take a moment to study her face, to have something to imagine later when I'm alone. "All right then." I lean over and kiss her cheek. "I love you." I dare to whisper in her ear.

She takes me by both sides of my face and holds me against her head. I close my eyes tight and feel her nod. How my heart does ache.

42

Ginny

"I'm so scared," I say to Livvie as we lay side by side.

I feel her turn towards me. "I know." She rubs my arm. "This is like old times, isn't it? Sharing a bed?"

I hear the smile in her tone and know she's wishing for me to think of anything other than my current circumstance.

I grin. "I suppose it is. This bed is a bit bigger and more comfortable than that mattress I had stuffed with grass at the cabin."

I pull the blankets up around my neck. "I sure do miss the fellas something terrible at times."

Livvie wraps her arm around me. "Tell me about you and Silas."

"What about me and Silas?" Heat rises in my face and I'm unsure if Livvie can see me or not. "Is it dark in here?" I realize I don't even know what time it is other than Doc and Miss Bea have retired for the night and we girls have washed up and dressed for bed.

"For the most part, yes. There's a little light shining in from the moon. I can see that you're beside me, but I can't see details." She gives me a gentle nudge. "So, Silas. Tell me."

"I don't know what to say. He's remained by my side." My body suddenly aches for his touch. "I miss him." Sadness fills my chest. "I should have stayed with him today instead of leaving the ranch so upset. I was angry and pushed the horse too hard. No one knows that part, but I don't remember falling."

Livvie squeezes my arm tenderly. "It's not your fault."

I recall Silas crying out to God when he thought I was asleep.

"Why do you believe this happened to me?"

She sighs. "I don't know."

The house creaks and the clock ticks.

The bed gives as Livvie props herself up with her elbow. "Perhaps it happened *for* you."

My heart races. "What does that mean?" What good could come of this?

"Sometimes things in life seem horrible. They feel like they're happening to us, but truly, they're happening for our own good."

I begin to protest, but Livvie goes on. "Please, let me explain. I thought my mother putting me out was the worst thing that could happen to me, but it protected me from her husband, and I made a new family with the women at the brothel. I believed Roy being killed and Wes demanding to marry me was the worst outcome, but it led me here, and to Justus. Do you understand how we can see life's circumstances differently?"

"I do, but I can't see the good right now, if there is any good to be had. I'm sorry."

The relentless tightening of my stomach doesn't waver.

"I understand, it will take time. But Ginny, Silas loves you so much. That is as clear as day. And I'm here for you. We'll do anything and everything we can to help you through this. All hope is not lost. You must believe that."

"I believe I need to try and rest now, Livvie."

I don't care to hear about hope.

My friend places a kiss on my cheek. "Good night, Ginny. I love you."

I love her too, but can't bring myself to say it in fear that I'll begin to cry. I roll over, snuggle with Naomi, and will myself to sleep.

When I wake, light is streaming through the window. It appears as though it's going to be a wonderful day.

Light! I see light. There's light. I can see. "Livvie, wake up." I shake my sleeping friend who I am able to see clearly lying beside me.

"Ginny?" Livvie yawns and stretches.

"I can see. This is a miracle." I shout before hopping out of the bed and doing a twirl. I go to the window and see, with my own eyes, the sun cresting the town. I see the leaves and the bark of the tree outside the window. "I must go tell Silas at once." I turn back towards the bed to see if Livvie is up. When I do, everything's gone back to pitch darkness. "Livvie, where are you? Livvie, I can't see you."

"Shhh, I'm right here. You're just having a bad dream." Livvie's holding me, we're still in bed, and I'm still blind.

It was a dream. A wonderful dream where I had sight once

more. Livvie holds me while I weep into her nightgown.

"It's time to eat breakfast, sleepy head." Livvie is sitting on the edge of the bed smoothing her hand over my hair. "And Doc wants to check on your wound after you eat."

"I'm not hungry." I've decided I'm done eating. I can't live like this.

"Honey, you must eat. You need your strength."

"For what? I can't do anything."

"Yes, you can. You *can* do anything. You can still walk, speak, hear, feel. You can still *love*."

Footsteps approach the doorway. "Good morning, ladies." It's Rebecca's voice I hear. "Breakfast is ready. I made pancakes, bacon, and eggs."

There's a smile in her tone that I long to see. I can imagine it in my mind because I remember it. But I can't truly see it, and that makes me angry.

My teeth grind and heat flushes through my body.

"Ginny, would you like me to bring you a plate, or are you feeling up to coming down to the kitchen?"

"I'm not hungry," I moan. I don't wish to be cruel to Rebecca, but I don't care to speak or eat.

"Let's bring her a plate. Perhaps she'll change her mind," Livvie says softly.

I won't change my mind. I refuse.

I hear Rebecca's steps retreating down the stairs.

Naomi slept beside me throughout the night, but now I can't find her. "Naomi?" I feel around the bed for her.

"I let her out," says Livvie.

"What if she runs off? She's not used to this house." Fear and panic fill me as I think of not having the cat with me, and what would Silas say?

A jolt of heat floods my body, my chest tightens, and every muscle quivers.

"She'll be fine. Now, Miss Bea has asked Rebecca to come take care of you during the day."

"I don't need to be taken care of." I know my eyes are open, but they see only darkness. I wonder if this is what hell feels like. I suppose when I die soon, I'll be prepared.

"Oh, Ginny, don't give her any trouble."

"If she leaves me alone there won't be any trouble." A vein pulses at the side of my head, and I grimace at the pain.

Rebecca returns with the smell of bacon and maple syrup that causes my stomach to rumble with hunger, but I refuse to feed it.

"Thank you, Rebecca," Livvie states. "I'll stay a bit longer. Ginny, Rebecca made a fine meal. You ought to give it a try."

I hear Livvie's footsteps as she moves from where Rebecca set the plate back around the bed, to where I lay. "Here, just one bite?"

Fury rages within me. This is all good and well for her, she has her eyesight. "Stop treating me like a child," I yell, bounding from the bed and in the process hit the plate and Livvie. I hear the shattering of the dish and Livvie's gasp.

The baby. I didn't mean to hit her, but I can't back down now.

I'm too enraged and ashamed of myself to admit wrongdoing. "I'll starve myself," I shout. "Leave me be." I slam my pounding head back down and pull the pillow over it then scream as loud as I can.

"I'm sure this is very hard for you, Ginny, but it doesn't give you a right to bite the hand that's trying to feed you. You know what? You're on your own. I'm going home." Livvie stomps from the room and down the stairs.

Angry at myself, and yet angry at Livvie, I sob under my pillow. No one understands because they can still see.

"Ginny?"

Shame washes over me at the sound of Doc's voice. I realize I must have fallen asleep.

"Let's take a look at your head."

I obey by sitting up against the headboard and composing myself. I must look a fright.

"Your head's still rather swollen. How's the pain?"

"Still quite uncomfortable."

"I want you to continue resting. Don't attempt the stairs just yet. That was quite a fall, and I'm afraid you've sustained a nasty concussion. You could also be in shock. It's difficult to determine the cause of your vision impairment, but I believe rest is the best course of action."

My anxiety hitches. "A concussion? What's that?" I grab at the covers.

Doc chuckles. "It's just a fancy way of saying you hit your head real hard." He pats my leg and leaves the room.

"Ginny, it's Rebecca here."

I turn my head toward the sound of her voice. "Rebecca?"

"Silas and Samuel brought a wash bin in your room so you can take a proper bath. It's not very big, but it'll do. Let's get you cleaned up."

An unpleasant odor wafts with my movements, and my hair is heavy with oil. Perhaps a bath will help.

Once washed and back in bed, fear still grips me, but I'm no longer angry. I can't be angry with these people who love me and are taking such good care of me.

"Oh, dear," says Miss Bea. "It's so good to see you all fresh faced as I'm used to."

I can imagine her bounding into the room staring at me with her hands clasped to her bosom.

"I brought you a cold pork sandwich, a slice of apple pie, and a glass of milk. I know breakfast didn't go so well, but Doc and I do insist you eat and not give Rebecca any trouble." Her voice is sweet but stern. I imagine Hannah's heard this tone a time or two. "Now, if you'll eat your dinner, I'll give you more medicine for your head. I prefer you have something on your stomach, so you don't vomit it up."

I understand now. They don't seek for me to be at ease with my condition, but rather, they wish for my body to heal.

"I'll eat." I feel the corner of my mouth lift. "Thank you, Miss Bea."

"Well, all right then. Rebecca, I'll be in the kitchen if you need me."

"Thank you, ma'am." I hear the creak of the rocking chair beside the bed as Rebecca sits in it.

"I was thinking," Rebecca says. "It must grow quite dull not having anything to do, so I thought I'd read to you if that's all right. Samuel bought me this book called *Little Women*. Can you believe it, Ginny, my very own book."

In my mind's eye, I can see Rebecca's beautiful smile.

"I sent him to the mercantile for sugar, and he brought me this book all wrapped up so nice in brown paper and string. He said Mister Jenkins was sitting them out and something told him I needed one." She giggles. "'Foolish man'," I said to him. "'When am I going to find time to read a whole book?' Well, I suppose someone knew better than me because here I am, about to read it to you, Ginny."

The chair creaks, and a moment later the bed gives under Rebecca's weight. "Would you like to feel it?"

I'm confused a moment, but then realize, maybe I would like to feel it. Sitting my plate aside I hold out my hands for the book. "Yes, thank you."

I run my palm over it. "I've never thought about how a book feels before. Is this the front?"

"It is."

"It's hard. It's not smooth but not entirely rough either. What color is it?"

"Green with gold lettering."

I trace my fingers over the rough edges of the paper and the gentle indentation where the binding lies. I open the book and run my fingers over each page as I turn them. "The pages are cream."

"Yes, they are."

"You say the title is, *Little Women*? What's the name of the author?"

"Louisa May Alcott."

"That's a pretty name." I hold the book out to hand it back to Rebecca. "I'd love for you to read it to me."

Taking my plate back up, I eat as Rebecca reads.

"Part 1 Playing Pilgrims. 'Christmas won't be Christmas without any presents,' grumbled Jo, lying on the rug."

"'It's so dreadful to be poor!' sighed Meg, looking down at her old dress…"

I find myself so lost in the story of Jo, Beth, and Meg, that I nearly forget all about the fact that I can't see. No, I can see. I can see in my mind.

It's been five days since my accident with the horse. I'm becoming more resolved to my new way of life. Doc still won't permit me to go down the stairs. Oh, how I would love to sit outside. But Rebecca opens my window and places me beside it in the rocker so I can feel the breeze and sun upon my face when the light falls just right. Silas has been here every day to see me and keep me company. I recount the story of the girls in Rebecca's book. That story has made me realize the importance of true love and what it means. I also realize behind every strong woman are other strong women. I think of the strong women behind me—

Rebecca, Miss Bea, Livvie. Oh, Livvie, I must apologize to her as soon as I'm able to leave this house.

Silas pats my hand. "She understands, Ginny. It's been hard for all of us, not just you. Your loss is our loss. Your heartbreak is our heartbreak, because we love you."

Naomi purrs in my lap. "I feel a bit overwhelmed, I must admit. I think I need rest now."

He places a kiss upon my cheek. "Of course. I'll be downstairs if you need me."

My first day in this room, Miss Bea had set a bell on the nightstand, beside me, in the event I needed something. I could ring it, and someone would come tend to me. That woman thinks of everything.

I settle in feeling so grateful for the people downstairs who love me and have been taking such good care of me. I find myself falling into a slumber with a smile on my face.

Coming out of my nap, I stretch and yawn. I declare, being cooped up in this room has made me lazy. All I do is sleep. But thankfully the headaches have lessened. I roll over and open my eyes and gasp. I see light and shadows. I knock the bell to the floor in an attempt to grab it and at the same time I yell, "Silas, Miss Bea, Rebecca." I get to the floor and feel for the bell, but I can't find it. "Someone, please come," I shout. I stand and am able to see enough light and shadows that I can carefully move between the rocker and bed to the door of the room. "Silas," I shout from the doorway.

"Ginny." Heavy boots thud up the stairs.

"What is it, dear?" Miss Bea is right behind him.

It's darker in the doorway, so I can't make out their shadows as clearly, but I laugh. "I can see."

Silas takes hold of my shoulders. "You can see?"

"I can't see you very well at the moment, but I can see light and shadows and if you step closer to the window, I'll be able to make out where you are."

"I'm going to fetch Doc," Miss Bea exclaims in excitement.

When she returns with Doc, he examines my eyes, asking me to follow his finger this way and that.

"You can't make out objects—just light and shadows?" he asks.

Silas takes my hand. "This is good news?"

"Well, seeing light and shadows is much better than seeing total darkness I'd say. How about you, Ginny?"

"Oh yes. I'm going to dress. Silas, will you help me down to the back garden?"

"Of course." There's elation in his voice.

Miss Bea claps her hands. "Oh, this calls for a celebration. Ginny, you'll have dinner at the table this evening, and afterward we'll have dessert on the porch."

"A bit of fresh air and dinner in the dining room is fine this evening, however I recommend that you continue to take it easy and avoid exerting yourself for the time being," Doc interjects.

Silas kisses my head, and I can't help but believe that if this hadn't happened, he wouldn't be here with me now. Perhaps Livvie was right. But also, what is worse, limited eyesight or living without the man I love?

43

Silas

Rebecca sits a cup of coffee in front of me and pats my shoulder before taking a seat across the table. "Are you still residing at the hotel?"

"Yes, I may be purchasing land from Justus. We've discussed it in the past but nothing's set in stone. I'd like to start building right away. But first, I need to make things right with the church."

"Are you still working for Bart Matthews?"

I nod as I swallow the drink that fills my mouth. Rebecca makes wonderful coffee. "He told me to take the remainder of the week off so I could be here for Ginny and get my affairs in order."

"I can't say I'm not disappointed in your deception, but I appreciate your confessing the truth. Also, I haven't thanked you for standing up for Samuel." Rebecca looks me tenderly in the eyes. "Thank you, Silas."

My scalp prickles and I clear my throat. "Samuel's a good

man. I couldn't stand by and watch him being treated badly."

"Thank you," she repeats, tears brimming in her eyes.

"I hear Livvie sent off another letter to the papers out East in search of your daughters."

"That Livvie is such a sweet soul. Yes, if only we are as blessed to receive news from them as I was with Samuel. Only time will tell I suppose. And if I'm unable to see them until I get to heaven, I guess that's how it must be."

The weight of Rebecca's pain is heavy on my chest as I sit here with her, and although her faith runs deep in the white man's God, I can't say as though I feel the same. I do, however, believe deeply in righting the wrongs.

I let out a deep breath just before opening the church door, knowing the Board awaits my arrival inside. This morning after speaking with Rebecca, and Ginny reassuring me that she was fine, I visited Mister McCalister, asking that he bring the members together. I knew of all the men, he'd be the most rational and could help me do this peacefully.

Justus insisted on accompanying me as he believes I need both an advocate and a witness in my corner. Samuel, too, stands at my side.

He and Rebecca had been attending services here, but when the blatant hypocrisy of Milton Brady became apparent, they began holding their own family services in their home. I didn't take it personally or blame them in the least.

Justus slaps a hand to my shoulder, and I take a step inside.

Mister McCalister stands and holds his hand out to me. "Silas." Then he does the same with Justus and Samuel, greeting them in kind.

I glance at the sheriff, who stands off to the side with his hands on his hips. They must be concerned that I'll land a blow on someone today.

Joseph Perry, wasting no time, clears his throat. "Silas, you called this meeting today. What do you have to say for yourself?"

"I have deceived the church, and I've come to repent for my transgressions."

I won't be recounting to them the entire story of my deception. That's between me, *my* God, those closest to me, as well as the young lady whose honor I protected, of course.

"It would be easy for me to take the coward's way out and leave town, but I have friends here and I plan to make Laurel Springs my home." I shift from one foot to the other. "You see, I'm not a minister. I haven't attended seminary school. I met the man who was to arrive as your pastor, but he had an accident and wasn't able to make it, so I used the opportunity to pretend I was him." I motion towards Justus and Samuel who remain seated in the pew beside me. "The Bennett and Peterson families have been so gracious as to forgive me for what I've done. I hope you will too. I shall even go so far as to come in during the next service and confess to the entire congregation."

Milton Brady, whose nose is bandaged, jumps to his feet. "This is an abomination." He pounds his fist into the air.

"Now, Brother Brady," says Mister McCalister. "The church

does call on our brothers and sisters to confess their sins and that's what he's doing. We *are* called to forgive in turn."

"It's an outrage and he can't be allowed to get away with it." Brady stomps his foot. "Sheriff, you need to arrest this man for posing as a clergyman."

The sheriff cocks an eyebrow at Milton Brady before shooting a look to Justus.

Justus rises beside me. "Arrest? Truly, Brady?"

"Sheriff, arrest this man. Not only has he pretended to be a preacher, but he also assaulted me," Brady demands.

The lawman moves forward. "I'm afraid, Justus, I do have cause to detain Rev…Mister Flynn."

44

Ginny

It's been a couple of weeks since my accident and my vision has returned, although slower than I'd hoped. My sight is rather blurry, but I can see fine, nonetheless. I consider it a miracle, but Doc says there are medical advances we know nothing of yet. He suggests I consider making a trip to Denver to visit a physician who specializes in the eyes. He believes a pair of spectacles would clear things up for me, but I'm optimistic that my eyesight will be restored to how it was before the accident. Besides, I can't leave until after Silas's trial.

Silas has been sitting in jail since confessing his crime to the church board, and although he did not handle matters as he ought, I've come to see that he's a good man, and that he truly loves and cares for me.

Since my accident, I've had to reflect more on the inside, what I think and feel and less on the outside, what I see. Things aren't always as they appear, and Silas is a perfect example of that.

Miss Bea, Rebecca, and Hannah have been a wonderful help to me while I've been healing. And thankfully, I had the opportunity to apologize to Livvie for how terrible I was to her when she was here last to care for me. We all do things, at some point, that we shouldn't. Thank goodness for those who can forgive us as she forgave me.

I pack a cold pork sandwich, spread with jam, a side of sliced cheese, an apple, two molasses cookies, and a small jar of milk. I'm hoping that taking this to Silas today will cheer him up. The sheriff hasn't allowed me to visit him on account of me being a woman and there being other men in his custody. He said it would cause too much excitement. However, he sent his deputy over this morning to let me know he only had Silas detained, and I could see him now.

"You better make it quick, though, because you never know when we'll have to bring someone in for being drunk and disorderly," says the young deputy.

The stench of the jail is almost unbearable with the scent of sweat mingled with the unpleasant odor of urine. I'm tempted to ask the sheriff how he can bear working in such conditions, but refrain, not wishing to cause Silas discomfort at my judgment. I hold my tongue, offering a quick 'thank you' when the sheriff opens the cell, quickly places the basket of food inside, and then locks the door behind him.

"I'll be around the corner at my desk if you need anything." The man twirls the keys in his finger as he disappears to the other side of the wall.

The cell is poorly lit, a faint light trickling in through a small window high up in the wall, barely enough to cast a shadow. I eye a privy pot and a cot with a thin mattress and a wool blanket. Silas's eyes are rimmed red and swollen, his neck is scruffy with new growth, and his hair is greasy and disheveled.

"Ginny." His smile is proof that he's pleased to see me. He reaches through the bars and slides a thumb over my cheek. "I've missed you."

"I've missed you too."

"You shouldn't have come though. I don't want you to see me like this." He glances down as he speaks. Shame. I can see it in his eyes and hear it in his voice.

"Oh, I *had* to visit you." I reach my hand through the bars and hold his face in my palm.

He shakes his head. "I truly am so sorry for all the pain I've caused."

"The important thing is that you've atoned for your wrongs, and from here on out…" I stare deeply into his eyes. "No more secrets."

He slowly moves his head from side to side. "No more secrets."

I motion to the basket still on the floor. "Are you hungry?"

"Famished." His stare is intense, and I know he's referring to needing something other than food.

I bite my lower lip as heat washes up from my groin. "When they let you out of here, I'll make sure you're fed proper," I whisper.

He smiles so wide I wish I could climb in there with him now.

Not sure of how much time we have together, I urge him to eat the food I brought.

"You put jam on my sandwich." He cocks his head in

awe. "It's delicious."

"Well, I know just how you like it." I am proud of myself for putting together a meal I know he'll enjoy.

"Yes, you do." He gives me a wink and warmth spreads up my face.

"How's your eyesight? Justus told me it's improved."

"It has, although still a bit blurry. Doc believes I need to make a trip to Denver to see a physician who specializes in the eyes so he can give me glasses."

"When they let me out of here that's the first thing we'll do." He takes another bite of his sandwich. "How's Naomi?"

"No need to worry, she's well cared for. She makes me feel close to you. And she and Raven, Miss Bea's new mouser, get along splendid."

"I'm happy to hear it."

The sheriff reappears with a small wooden stool. "Here you are, Miss, it's not much, but it ought to be more comfortable than standing." He thumps the chair beside me.

"Thank you."

He tips his hat and rounds the corner out of sight.

"Do you know when they'll release you?" I ask Silas, who sits on the cot devouring his sandwich.

He chews the food and swallows quickly. "Justus has retained a lawyer for me."

"Yes, I heard."

"Did you hear that impersonating a clergyman could mean years of imprisonment?"

I chuckle. "That's preposterous."

Silas's solemn countenance lets me know he's not jesting.

I gasp. "Silas."

He rubs the apple on his breeches. "If that happens, Ginny, I want you to go on with your life."

I grab at the bars of the cell. "No. I'll wait for you, however long it takes."

He rests his elbows on his knees studying the fruit he twirls in his hand. "I couldn't bear it."

"When Jake passed, I was certain I'd follow him. But then things shifted, and now I find myself desiring to live more than ever. I wish to live — for Livvie, for Lenny, and for you. There are times when I've wondered if I should, but the pull I feel toward you is like that of a moth to a flame. So, if you think for one moment, Silas Flynn, that I will not wait for you, no matter the span of time, you are sorely mistaken."

Silas is now staring up at me and I realize I'm gripping the bars so tight my fingers have turned white. I loosen my hold.

He shakes his head and bellows.

My mouth's agape and I release the bars. "What's so humorous?"

"Woman." He reaches through the cell, takes my chin, and draws me in. "You try my patience."

His kiss is insistent, claiming my lips with all the force of his desire.

45

Ginny

This is the second day of Silas's trial, which has been held in a vacant building. A 'For Rent' sign adorns the front window. Pews have been brought in from the church, along with desks for the witness stand and the judge's bench.

There were many witnesses, most of whom had no true connection to the matter. Take Bridget Murphy, for example, who spoke of Silas and me, though I know she never once saw us together, except for that one night we danced during the reunion celebration that Justus and Livvie hosted for Samuel and Rebecca.

My heart pounds as I hold my breath waiting for Judge Yates to give his ruling. Lenny and Livvie sit on either side of me holding my sweaty hands. I stare at Silas, who gives no indication of his thoughts as the judge speaks.

"Silas James Flynn." The judge glares at Silas.

I squeeze Livvie and Lenny's hands. "

"I hereby sentence you to one year of hard labor at the Colorado Territorial Prison, where you shall remain for the duration of your sentence." The judge slams his gavel on the table and audible gasps fill the room.

I rush to Silas, who meets me with pained apologetic eyes as the sheriff places cuffs on his wrists.

Tears stream down my face as I take Silas's face in my hands. "I love you, and I'll be right here waiting for you." My lip quivers as I kiss him on the mouth.

"I'm so sorry, Ginny."

The sheriff pulls him away. "Come on, son, you have a long trip ahead of you."

"I'll write to you." I reach for Silas as he's led away. Justus wraps his arms around me and holds me while I release all the fear, worry, and anticipation of the outcome that I've been holding onto for weeks.

It's been a week since Livvie had the baby, and Lenny and I are riding to the ranch together to see the new addition to the Bennett family. I've longed to visit something fierce, but I've been mindful to give Livvie and Justus time to settle into their new roles as parents.

I saw Justus in town on Wednesday and sent word that we'd be visiting today so that our visit wasn't a surprise to Livvie.

It's been an exceptionally hot July, so Lenny and I are making the trip in the early morning before the sun becomes too oppressive.

To my surprise, Livvie greets us at the front door with her hair neatly plaited and wearing a flowery dress. Her cheeks are rosy, and her smile as lovely as ever.

"She's sleeping," Livvie whispers pointing towards the front room, and the three of us silently scream and hug with excitement so as not to wake the child.

"Come in. I have been just thrilled since Justus informed me you two would be visiting this morning." We follow her to the sitting room where she shows us to a bassinet by her rocker.

"Oh, Livvie, she's just darling," I whisper.

The wee one sleeps, swaddled in a blanket. Her head is covered in no more than fuzz like that of a peach. I study her tiny lips that move as she makes a small sucking motion. Four tiny fingers lay over the edge of her blanket as though she's holding onto it. Her nails are so scant I can hardly believe my eyes.

"She better wake before I leave here or I'm just going to snatch her right out of this bed," Lenny threatens.

Livvie chuckles. "I have fresh coffee on the stove, and Rebecca made us cinnamon cake."

We follow her to the kitchen, leaving the sleeping baby girl to her time in dreamland.

The kitchen is clean and quiet, and the fragrance of coffee wraps me in a comforting hug.

Livvie cradles her steaming cup in her hands. "Now, fill me in on all the town gossip. I must know all the details."

Lenny and I glance at one another and her shoulders drop with a sigh.

Livvie sits taller. "What is it?" Her eyes move between me and Lenny.

"Jesse's married." Lenny pokes at her slice of cake.

"How did you find out?"

"I traveled up to Boulder to deliver a ball gown for a lady of means who lives there. A gown she meant to take back East." Lenny waves her hand, as though dismissing the matter. "She insisted on collecting it from me herself, but I haven't been away from Laurel Springs in such a stretch that I offered to bring it to her." Lenny gestures towards me. "Ginny accompanied me."

"And this woman's his wife?" Livvie's now leaning into the table.

"No. We delivered the dress then decided to make a stop at the mercantile to look at their fabrics. As we were studying them, a small girl, about the age of five perhaps, was calling with excitement, 'Pa. Pa.' I didn't think anything of it until she ran into me, and I turned to find him standing there smiling down at her. When he noticed me, his face was that of a frightened pathetic fawn."

"Oh, Len." Livvie places her hand over her heart. "Did you say something to him?"

"I couldn't. I was stunned silent. Still staring at me, he tells the girl, 'Go see if you can find a book, Catherine, and Pa shall be right there.'"

Lenny inhales sharply blinking back tears.

"He reached his hand out to me." Lenny shifts in her chair. "As if he thought I'd take it. Isn't that something?" she scoffs. "He called my name, but I told the lovely woman who'd been helping us look at fabric that we appreciated her time, but we needed to catch our ride. Which was a falsehood, of course, because I rented a team from Clint. Then I walked past him without saying a word or looking at him."

"Did he follow you or call out for you?" Livvie inquires.

"No. How could he with his daughter in there, not old enough to be alone."

"I suppose you're right. When did this happen?"

Lenny sniffles. "Last week, Saturday. The fault is mine, truly. I ought to have kept it to business. Foolish me, I up and fell in love when I had no right."

"I'm sorry, Lenny," I say. "But married men shouldn't be intimate with public women." I'm only reminding her of what I've already expressed, but I feel it's worth repeating. Why, I don't know. I suppose I ought to say nothing. It's like rubbing salt on a wound.

"No, they shouldn't," Livvie echoes. "But I understand, it's just business and it's not your responsibility to make sure they're not taken."

Small cries make their way into the kitchen and Livvie smiles. "Well, I can promise you this," she pushes up from the chair. "Nothing will make you feel better than the sweet cuddles of a newborn babe."

When she returns, the child is cradled to Livvie's chest. "Isabella Rose, meet your aunties." Raising her arm and pulling the blanket away from the baby's face she says, "This is Aunt Ginny, and this is Aunt Lenny."

"Are we able to hold her?" I ache to get my hands on her.

"I dare say she's hungry." Livvie sits back in her chair at the table then glances at me and Lenny. "I don't think I need to cover myself in front of you ladies, do I?"

Lenny shooes her. "Of course not, hang those titties out, Mama."

I watch my friend feeding her sweet baby girl, and I can't help but recall the one Jake and I lost. I can't help but wonder if that will ever be me. If I'll ever have a child of my own. A twinge of jealousy niggles at me, but not for long, because Livvie deserves this life that she has. She's been through so much and I'm truly happy for her.

"Virginia." Livvie's snapping her fingers at me, and I realize I've been lost in thought. I giggle that she's treating me like a strict tutor I had as a child.

"I apologize, I was just thinking about how blessed you are and I'm so happy for you." My smile broadens.

"Thank you." Livvie holds her breast in her hand while peering down at her baby. "How are you, Ginny?"

"I'm well. Doing my best without Silas. I've received two letters from him. His spirit seems well. Although I'm certain if it weren't, he wouldn't tell me because he wouldn't wish for me to be concerned. I still am. And when I find myself tempted to complain about a simple inconvenience, I'm reminded that he's doing hard labor at a prison almost two days' journey away."

Livvie pats her feeding child. "Justus received a letter from him and stated the same thing. He must keep his head up to survive, and he doesn't want us fretting over him."

I nod. "I write to him every day, keeping him apprised of the town gossip, of course, and how Lenny has kept me busy.

And I just adore my apartment above the Schneider and Shulz Law Firm. When you're feeling up to it, you and Isabella must visit me."

"We will be thrilled to do that." Livvie pulls the baby from her breast. "Now, who would like to hold her first?"

"Me." Lenny and I call in unison.

46

Silas

1874 (July) Canon City, Colorado Territory

I step out of the Colorado Territorial Prison in the same garments I arrived in a year ago and fifty of the nearly 400 letters Ginny sent. The law sure saw to it that I had a ride here, but how I would make my way back home to Laurel Springs was of no concern to them. When Justus learned of my release, he wrote to say he would come for me. I could have easily taken the stagecoach or a train but seeing him waiting for me fills my heart with gladness, and I let out a whoop thrusting my fist into the air.

Justus wraps his arms around me and laughs. "It's good to see you, my friend."

With a racing heart I let out another whoop. "I'm a free man."

Justus claps a hand to my shoulder. "Come on, we better get moving. It's going to take a couple of hours to get back to the hotel, and I'm hungry."

The feeling of freedom is one of both elation and fear. I've spent the last year being told when to rise, when to eat, when to rest, and how I ought to be and not be. I'll need to begin thinking for myself again. Will Ginny still desire me, I wonder? I know I'm not the same person I was a year ago when I arrived in this place. My scars alone are proof of that. I clench my eyes at the thought of the abuse I endured here.

Justus speaks of the war changing him, but he's still a good man. If I can be half the man he is, I suppose I've turned out all right.

When we pull into the livery with the rented team, I notice that all about me, there are folks going about their daily tasks with no mind of who I am or where I just come from. The only thing I've seen for the last year are other men wearing the same garments as me, eating the same fare, and laboring in the harsh desert climate.

My cheeks burn, and I swallow hard against the tightness in my throat as I watch Justus pay for the team of horses. I long for a bath, a proper meal, and the comfort of a real bed. The man I was—convict—dies here and now.

Justus glances at this pocket watch before tucking it back into his denim breeches. "We still have two hours before they serve the midday meal. Why don't you settle into your room, and I'll meet you in the restaurant at noon?"

I tip my head. "Sounds good, my friend."

"Silas," Ginny cries as I step into the hotel room.

I drop my bag, wrap her in my arms, and twirl her around. "Oh, my sweet Ginny." Tears well in my eyes at the welcomed surprise of seeing her.

She cries and kisses all over my unshaven face. "I've missed you."

"I've missed you too." I set her down and allow my eyes to take her in. "You're truly here. I didn't—"

"I told Justus to keep it a surprise."

I chuckle. "You certainly have surprised me."

"Come," she says. "Let's get you a hot bath."

I rest my head on the back of the tub and close my eyes while Ginny brushes the sponge over my chest. "Of all the dreams I've had about this day, none compare to how it's turned out," I sigh.

Her hand stills. Peeking up, I see her eyes glisten with unshed tears. I lean in and lift her chin, gently pressing my mouth to hers.

"It's over now," I reassure her.

She wraps her arms around my neck and her lips part for my tongue that begs to be let in. Heat builds in me as her tongue entwines with mine in a demanding dance and the possessive urge to have her now grows.

"Take off your clothes."

Without a word, she unbuttons her blouse, still on her knees at the tub.

As I dry off, I watch her remove her garments and think of how I've never felt for anyone the way I feel for her. My heart hurts at how much she means to me. "Ginny Price," I take her by the waist. "I'm so in love with you."

She leans in and lays a soft kiss on my chest. "And I with you, Silas Flynn."

Those words from her lips are like fuel to the fire of passion that rages within me. "Oh, my sweet Ginny."

I guide her to the bed where I bury my face in her breasts, kissing, sucking. Oh, how I've longed to touch them. She whimpers softly as I make my way down her stomach to the warmth between her legs. I take a moment to study every curve and outline of her wet, pink flesh. Slowly I insert a finger watching it move in and out. She opens her legs wider.

"Oh, Silas."

I run my tongue along her inner thigh and kiss it before moving to the beautiful swollen bud that begs for my attention. I lick and suck at it, slipping another finger into her tight entrance. She bucks at me as I move them in and out.

"Damn it, Silas."

I love hearing my name on her tongue while I'm pleasuring her, and I smile to myself as I suck harder and move my glistening fingers faster.

"Yes, oh yes." She bucks quicker.

My fingers find their way to her hardened nipples, and I knead them firmly.

She balls the blanket into her fists as short breaths escape her body. "I'm almost there. I'm almost there. Oh, Silas."

I suck and nibble with more pressure at her needy mound.

"Oh, Silas. Damnit, I love you." Her body jolts as though struck by lightning. I remove my fingers so I can suck every last drop of her juices from her beautiful flesh that I am able to lap up as her body eases back down from the pleasurable peak she ascended.

Once I'm certain she's been fully satisfied, I kiss my way up her body before pushing my throbbing shaft into her. Grabbing her outer thigh and lifting, I rasp, "Say it again."

"I love you."

"Say it again." I need to hear those words as I fill her with every inch of me.

"I love you, Silas," she repeats, breathlessly. "I love you. I need you. I long for you."

"Oh, Ginny, I love you, and I love the way you feel on the inside. I don't ever want this to end." Nothing around me exists except this woman before me. Her breasts move with every plunge I make into her and her golden hair cascades around her face and down her shoulders. I'm truly the most fortunate man alive at this moment, I just know it.

The pressure builds as I reach the crest of bliss. I moan into the room as my body thrums.

After regaining my breath, I hold myself above her studying every part of her face. "I never forgot your smile, not one single day. That's what helped me through the last year. Your smile and your letters."

This makes her grin.

Her arms clasp around my neck and she draws me in for a kiss. As her hands slide down my back, a look of alarm flashes on her face. "What's on your back?"

"What do you mean?" I don't feel anything other than her hands.

She sits up, shoves me down, then gasps in horror. That's

when I realize she's just noticing my scars.

"They did that to you?" Her hand covers her mouth.

I bring her into my arms. "It's over now," I remind her.

"But—"

"Shhh…it's over." I don't wish to recall the torment I lived through in that place, not for a moment.

Her face is wet when I kiss her cheek.

"I'm so sorry," she whispers.

"There's nothing for you to be sorry about, sweetheart. I bore my punishment and it's now behind me."

She nods, and I kiss her lips, then her cheek, and the tip of her nose.

It doesn't take long for me to grow hard against her, our naked bodies tangled together, and the love we have for one another wrapped around our hearts.

I moan into her mouth as I slide my fingers between her very wet legs. They glide easily and quickly over her most sensitive spot.

"Oh, Silas," she groans into the room, spreading her legs for me.

She opens even wider as I work her soaked and swollen bud.

"That's it," I breathe into her ear.

Looking down the length of her body past her beautiful breasts I watch my fingers move vigorously.

She slides her leg over my body further opening herself up as she moves against my hand.

I turn my eyes to the pleasure on her face as my fingers continue to move swiftly. Her eyes are closed, and I know she's taking in every sensation of my hand, satisfying her need to be touched. She wets her lips with her tongue, and I have a sudden need to feel those lips wrapped around my aching erection.

Her head turns towards me, drawing her mouth to mine. Our kiss is heated and untamed as I continue to work her dripping flower.

"Don't stop. Don't stop. I'm almost there," she breathes against my lips.

I smile, watching her flail about in sheer bliss, her breasts bouncing joyfully.

"Yes. Yes. Yes." The room fills with her cries of pleasure. And my heart feels as if it shall burst with the love I have for this magnificent woman.

I hold her, never ever wishing to let her go.

47

Ginny

Silas has taken up residence at the ranch because he's now overseeing Bennett's Feed Mill and Blacksmith, which Justus built over the last year. The operation quickly put Milton Brady out of business.

Justus's response when he saw a for sale sign at Brady's was, "That's what you call a causality. His actions brought about his own loss. Had he acted more wisely his fate might've been different."

I can't argue with his point.

Since it's Sunday, neither Silas nor I have work, so I've come to the ranch for dinner and to spend time with my love who's been home a little over a month now. I don't wish to push him, but I'm beginning to wonder if we'll be more than what we are, mere lovers. It's understood that we'll be together for years to come, yet there's been no discussion of marriage or starting a family, and I find myself uncertain of how I ought to feel about that.

Little Isabella wiggles in Livvie's lap. "She's crawling all over the place now. I'm continuously worried about her burning herself on the stove or climbing the stairs then falling down them."

I clap my hands and hold them to the baby whose hair has grown into a soft little mohawk. "Bella, do you wish to come to Aunt Ginny?"

She giggles and holds her arms out. Livvie passes her to me from across the table and I squeeze the dear child in my arms. She lays her head against my chest and sucks on her chubby fist.

Silas runs a finger over Isabella's cheek. "She sure loves you."

I smile.

"Almost as much as I do."

My chest hitches at his words.

"Well," says Livvie. "She may be loving you even more in about six months, because she won't be receiving as much of my attention as she does now." Livvie rubs her belly.

"Are you…" I glance to Justus who's grinning from ear to ear then back to Livvie who curls her lips into a cheshire smile.

"What can I say," Justus twirls a spoon on the table. "My gun's got lots of powder."

I laugh at the recollection of Mirna telling Livvie some men have no powder in their gun.

After dinner, Livvie takes the baby upstairs for a nap, and I begin clearing the table with Silas's help. He's always ready to lend a hand. There is no men's work or women's work with him, and it's one of the many things I love about him.

"I'd like to take you for a ride," he says.

"A ride?"

"Yes, It's a gorgeous day. What do you say?"

"All right," I respond with excitement.

Since Silas has been home from prison he's taken me for a couple of rides. We had a picnic once at the lake, and another time we explored one another's bare bodies in a rift among the boulders. I imagine this is his plan for today and the corner of my mouth twitches at the thought of his touch.

"Are we going into town?" I ask when I realize we're heading in that direction.

"No ma'am," there's playfulness in his voice.

"Then where are you taking me, Silas Flynn?" I give his arm a squeeze.

"You'll see soon enough." He slides his arm around me and draws me close. "Now tell me, what's been the best part of your day?"

"Seeing you, of course." I lay my head on his shoulder but quickly right myself due to the bumpiness of the ride.

"Ahh, seeing you is the best part of my day as well."

Evergreens and aspens line the road and a squirrel scurries in front of the wagon then back. The horses are moving slow enough that the little guy, or gal, won't get hurt and that puts my mind at ease.

Silas nudges my shoulder. "What have you missed most since moving to Laurel Springs?"

"The fellas?"

"Besides them."

"I've missed living in the country where I can hear nothing but the wolves howling at night and the wind rustling the trees in the day." I think about what else I've missed. I've missed the fellas and Mirna immensely. I push past the thickness in my throat. "Buck," I shout. "I've missed Buck sorely. And Mister Harold as well."

"I still can't believe how much you love that mangy cat." Silas shakes his head.

I give him a nudge. "He is as sweet as honey."

"I don't know about all that," his voice is laced with doubt.

Not far past the ranch, Silas leads the team through a grove of thick trees that open into a clearing.

I peer around. "And what exactly do you have planned here, Mister Flynn?" I rub his thigh, joyful to be completely alone with him.

"You'll see."

He guides me down and away from the wagon. "Watch your step, there's large rocks and prairie dog holes."

I take his arm and squeeze. "You wouldn't let me fall."

"No, I wouldn't." He pats my hand.

The sun dips towards the shadowed mountains. There's a gorgeous view of the range from here, with boulders jutting out like jewels adorning the queen's crown.

"How are you feeling, Ginny?"

"About?"

"Everything. Anything. Your health? Life?"

"I'm thankful I have you and our friends. I'm thankful my

eyesight has been fully restored and that you're home."

"Am I home though?" He casts a puzzled look.

My eyebrows furrow. "What do you mean? Of course you're home. Isn't Laurel Springs your home now?" My heart rate picks up in fear he's bringing me here to deliver bad news. All the time I waited for him, and he's going to leave me.

Silas takes me in his arms and draws me close, our bodies pressed against one another. "I have something for you."

"A gift?"

He pushes a cloth wrapped in ribbon into my hand. "Go ahead and open it."

I know that it's something small but can't make out what it is. When I untie the string a metal piece falls out into my palm. "A thimble."

"You remember the first night we met we played hide the thimble."

The memory brings laughter to my belly. "Yes, how could I forget?"

"Ginny, that evening, meeting you, changed my life forever. That has been the single most important day of my life thus far. For so long I lived with no purpose but to survive. Then I met you, and all of that changed. You've made me a better man, a man who wishes to stay in one place, with one woman. If you'd never regained your eyesight, I would still love you with everything I have in me."

He lowers himself to one knee before me and takes my hands in his. "Virginia Price, I know this a lot to ask, and we can take as long as you wish, but—"

"Yes." I squeal.

"What?"

"Yes, yes, yes." I take his face in my hands.

"So, you'll take that thimble and sew me a new shirt?" His eyes widen in delight.

I swat him and we both laugh.

"Ginny, will you be my wife and live with me here on this property?"

"What?" My body trembles. "This is your property?"

"I'm purchasing 40 acres from Justus, on payments, no interest." He stands and wraps his arms around my waist. "It's *our* property, if you'll be my wife."

I clasp my arms around his neck. "Virginia Flynn," I muse, glancing up through my lashes, contemplating how the name sounds.

"*Missus* Virginia Flynn." Silas tugs me closer for a deep and lingering kiss.

48

Ginny

1875 (February)

"Charlotte is a beautiful name, Livvie." I perch on the edge of my friend's bed swaddling her new baby girl.

"I named her after a very dear friend from a long time ago." Livvie's smile suggests sadness and I recall her telling me of her friend Charlotte, who died in her arms at a brothel.

"It's a beautiful name, Livvie, for a beautiful child."

"Have you considered names?"

I caress my now expanding waistline. "We've been discussing possibilities."

Charlotte sleeps peacefully tucked into my arm and my stomach is large enough to give her a place to rest. "When I had my accident, Rebecca read Little Women by Louisa May Alcott to me. I believe Louisa May would be fitting if we were to have a daughter."

Livvie pulls her blanket taut. "That is a lovely name."

"Mama's baby." Bella runs into Livvie's room pointing to me while making it clear that Charlotte did not belong to me.

"Aunt Ginny can hold Mama's baby, Bell."

"Oh, dear." Mary scoops Bella up. "I do apologize, she snuck right up those stairs from under my nose."

Livvie and I chuckle as Mary leaves the room with the little girl and the promise of a cookie if she stays downstairs.

"That child is as quick as a whip." Livvie shakes her head. "Thank goodness I have Mary to help me."

I gently hand the baby back to Livvie. "I believe I've overstayed my welcome."

"Nonsense," Livvie murmurs, tucking the child into her arm.

I sway my hips from side to side stretching them. "My body would argue otherwise."

"How are you doing, other than feeling spent?" Livvie snuggles down with the baby beside her.

"My back hurts and it's hard to get sleep. I don't understand sometimes how my poor husband puts up with me."

Livvie giggles. "I know exactly what you mean. I wish I could tell you it gets easier, but that baby will continue to get bigger."

"I know," I sigh.

"He or she will be here before you know it, so try and get as much rest as you're able."

"I will." I kiss Livvie's cheek and pull back Charlotte's blanket to sneak one last peek. "I'd kiss her too, but I don't wish to wake her. And I believe you're the one who ought to be resting now."

The past months have gone in a blur with much change.

So many came out to help us with our barn raising—Justus, Samuel, Clint, Bart, Calvin, George, and more. Once the barn was complete, we had a beautiful outdoor wedding ceremony and a celebration inside. It didn't take long after for our house to be finished. And Silas hasn't slowed down since.

Justus offered him a partnership into the feed mill and blacksmith shop. The business was soon renamed Bennett and Flynn Feed and Smithing. Not long after, Silas purchased a gelding and a mare from Clint, which we now call Duke and Duchess.

I didn't mind living in the apartment in town, but Silas was adamant that he didn't want the baby to be born while we lived in such a small space, and above a law firm at that, certain they'd boot us out for the crying alone.

When I ride into the yard, Duchess and I are met by an excited Buck, who trails me to the barn then into the house after I stable the horse.

Since I spend most of my time in the kitchen cooking and baking, Silas placed the room so that I can see out onto the mountain range. I often think of Old Man Marshall, Tucker, Lee, and the others and wish them many blessings.

I still love Jake, and at times find myself in tears over missing him and what we had together. It's possible, I've come to learn, that you are able to love two men at the same time but in different ways. I love Jake for what we had. He and I grew up together and over the years had many experiences and met many challenges. I love Silas for what we have now. And I understand now that I haven't sought to use him as a replacement for Jake. No one could ever take Jake's place.

A tear slips down my cheek and I use my sleeve to wipe it away. "I love you, Jake."

I love you too, Ginny.

It's been a long time since I've heard him whisper in my ear, and it brings a smile to my face knowing he's still with me when I need him, just as Mirna had said he would be.

I glance to the teapot and cups that were a gift from my friend. I keep them in the hutch Silas had made for me as a wedding gift. Mirna gave me more than the tea set, I realize. She gave me the gift of her friendship, knowledge, and the beautiful stone that still hangs about my neck. I place my hand over it and close my eyes. "Thank you, Mirna."

Buck howls as I pull the pot roast from the oven, and I know that Silas has made it home safely.

Although I miss working side by side with Lenny, I wouldn't trade spending my days here on our homestead for anything. I've done well making extra earnings on the side for myself by bottling dried herbs and tinctures and selling them at Jenkins Mercantile.

"We ought to open you your own apothecary. You'd make more money off your goods than you do selling them to Harold Jenkins," Silas has suggested.

"At the present, I'm content spending my days here at home. Perhaps later when the baby grows older, we can give the matter further thought."

Buck wags his tail at Silas who enters the kitchen with a smile. "It smells wonderful in here."

He removes his hat and coat, warms his hands at the stove,

then wraps his arms around me from behind, caressing my belly and kissing my exposed neck, which send tingles to my toes. "How's my stunningly beautiful, pregnant wife today?" he moans in my ear as he moves his hands from my belly to my breasts.

I bite my lip, finding it hard to slice the loaf of bread. "You better be careful, Silas Flynn, or you'll end up having dessert before supper."

"Oh, but that's precisely what I want." He slowly pulls the strings of my apron allowing them to fall gently, one…two. The smock drops to my feet, and he unbuttons my blouse while laying a trail of kisses over my neck.

My knees weaken, and I release the knife on the counter and tilt my head giving him full access to the sensitive skin below my ear.

"Once the baby arrives, I won't be able to love on your voluptuous body anywhere or anytime I please." He cups my throat, tipping my head back and laying his mouth on mine. I reach around and feel over the hard bulge in his pants.

"My sweet, sweet Ginny. How did I get so lucky?" he breathes into my lips.

"I love you, Silas."

He plunges his tongue into my mouth then pulls away. "Say it again," he whispers.

"I love you," I murmur.

"I love you too, sweetheart."

Silas and I arrived in this town separately, for different purposes, and under different circumstances. Little did we know at the time, we were both on a path to answering love's call.

Author's Note

Thank you so much for taking the time to read Silas and Ginny's story. As an indie author, I truly rely on your support. If you enjoyed the book, I would be so grateful if you could leave a review on StoryGraph, BookBub, or wherever you purchased it. Share your thoughts on social media and request your library purchase a copy.

If you create a positive post about this book, please make sure to tag me! Positive reviews, emails, and DMs really keep us authors going, so don't hesitate to let us know when you love our work.

You can find me on Instagram at @amandajspeights, and on TikTok and BlueSky at @amandaspeights. Also, don't forget to sign up for my newsletter at www.AmandaSpeights.com to stay updated on Book 3 of my Laurel Springs series!

Acknowledgements

Ted, my amazing husband and muse, I wouldn't be where I am today without your belief in me. You're my biggest supporter, and I love you for it. Thank you for reminding me that everything I want is on the other side of fear.

Mila, my beautiful daughter, inside and out. I find it funny when you come into my office, plop into the chair, and ask, "Whatcha doin'?" or "How's you're life?" Please don't ever stop doing that. ♥

To our Colorado friends, you know who you are: I so appreciate your support—purchasing my books, reading my stories, and supporting my author signings.

H.H. Rune, my dear friend and fellow indie author, whether we're working or just chatting, I'm so grateful for you and our Zoom calls. Some days, your accountability is what keeps me going.

Blake Burns, my fellow smutty romance author buddy, thank you for reading the very rough draft of Silas and Ginny's story and offering your input. I hope my changes receive your stamp of approval.

Brittany, my editor, I truly appreciate your insightful feedback and your help in getting this story ready to share with the world.

My incredible cover designer, Roseanna White, at www. roseannawhitedesigns.com, once again, you've created something absolutely stunning. Thank you for bringing my vision to life.

My Women's Fiction Indie Author Group, I am so thankful for all of you. The support and knowledge within our little group have been invaluable, and you've played a huge part in my growth as an author.

Finally, thank you to my readers and those who do such an amazing job lifting me up. You keep me going on those days when I'm struggling, reminding me why I'm doing this..

About the Author

Historical Western Romance author Amanda Speights weaves spicy tales of resilient women and bold adventures from her home at the foot of America's Mountain, where she lives with her husband and daughter. Though her grown son, daughter-in-law, and three sweet-and-sour grandsons live 1,300 miles away, they are always close in her heart. Her passion for storytelling shines through her work, celebrating the Old West's timeless spirit. Amanda invites her readers to saddle up and journey through love stories that are as enduring as the Rocky Mountains themselves.

Her debut novel, Love's Arrival, is the first book in the Laurel Springs series, set in the Colorado Territory during the late 1800s. Amanda loves engaging with her readers and offers a newsletter, which can be found at www.AmandaSpeights.com, to keep fans informed about her latest releases and book news. Followers can also connect with her on Instagram at @AmandaJSpeights, and on TikTok and BlueSky at @AmandaSpeights.

Amanda divides her time between crafting her latest historical romance, homeschooling her daughter, and immersing herself in period fiction that spotlights formidable women.

Author photo: © Melissa DeMers Photography

Other Books by Amanda Speights

In 1872, life can change as unexpectedly as the prairie winds.

Livvie McLain has always dreamed of the kind of love she read about in her grandparents' letters, filled with longing and devotion. Nevertheless, she believes her mother's prophecy — that she wasn't born with that kind of fortune. When she falls for the ruggedly handsome and charming cowboy, Justus Bennett, Livvie finds herself in a dilemma. She fears he must be too good to be true and that she is unworthy of him.

Justus has spent the last six years consumed by the demands of his inherited family ranch — the same ranch he once swore he would never return to. Now, he's ready for love, but he's all but given up on finding the right woman to share his life with. When Olivia Palmer — Livvie McLain — stumbles into his life, he knows immediately that she's the one he wants to build a future with.

However, Livvie's tangled web of secrets, including the man she dared to escape, threatens to shatter any hope they have for a life together.

Content warnings: open door, domestic violence, sexual assault, abortion, miscarriage, death

This Page is Intentionally Left Blank

This Page is Intentionally Left Blank